"This Is Insane."

"What's insane about wanting a child?" Marsh stood, and came to lean against her side of the table. He was close—too close.

Jen had to raise her head to look at him. "Nothing," she said. "It's your way of going about it that's strange." Jen stared at him a moment, torn between wanting to shut him down—and wanting to go upstairs with him so she could have his mouth on hers again. Finally she asked, "Are you nuts?"

Rather than the anger she expected, Marsh treated her to his insides-melting laugh.

"I like you," he said. "You're as prickly as I am. I believe we could make a go of it."

"Of what? A marriage of convenience?" Jen somehow managed to keep her voice calm.

"Yes." He nodded.

"Whose?"

"What do you mean, *whose?*" He appeared perplexed.

"My convenience...or yours?"

Dear Reader,

Hi friends. It seems like forever since last I wrote to you. I've been on a sabbatical for some time (actually, I tell myself and everyone else who might ask, that I'm semi-retired). But it only works for a period of time before ideas for another story—or stories—begin knocking on my mind, demanding my attention.

The book you are holding in your hand is the first to tickle my interest. It began innocently enough with a title... *Beguiling the Boss*. Big deal, I mocked. I should have known better. Before too long I had characters vying for attention. Hmm, I mused...maybe. I started writing and, as always, ever since the first book I wrote, the characters led the way, telling me their story as I soon, and again as always, followed along. As I'm a hunt-and-pick typist, many times I simply could not keep up. Then, piqued, I would walk away until they—the hero or heroine—allowed me breathing room by slowing up a bit.

But all things considered, I supposed the characters must be right, because you, dear readers, appear to like the tales they tell me. I hope you will enjoy this particular story, as these two characters are both strong-willed and independent. Matter of fact, I found them to be rather beguiling.

Yeah, I know, I'm shameless, but the idea here is to catch your attention so you'll buy the book!

Thank you for all the years we've spent together through the pages of my books.

Yours always,

Joan Hohl

JOAN
HOHL

BEGUILING THE BOSS

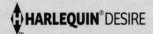

Recycling programs
for this product may
not exist in your area.

ISBN-13: 978-0-373-73228-9

BEGUILING THE BOSS

Copyright © 2013 by Joan Hohl

Printed in U.S.A.

www.Harlequin.com

Books by Joan Hohl

Harlequin Desire

Beguiling the Boss #2215

Silhouette Desire

*Wolfe Waiting #806
*Wolfe Watching #865
*Wolfe Wanting #884
*Wolfe Wedding #973
  A Memorable Man #1075
  The Dakota Man #1321
  A Man Apart #1640
*Maverick #1718
  The M.D.'s Mistress #1892
  In the Arms of the Rancher #1976

*Big, Bad Wolfe

Other titles by this author available in ebook format.

JOAN HOHL

is a bestselling author of more than sixty books. She has received numerous awards for her work, including a Romance Writers of America Golden Medallion award. In addition to contemporary romance, this prolific author also writes historical and time-travel romances. Joan lives in eastern Pennsylvania with her husband, Marv, and their family consisting of: two daughters, Lori and Amy, two grandchildren, Erica and Cammeron, and three great-grandsons, Jaden, Kieran and Sorin.

To my own "Gang"...six writers from various parts of the country, all of us different in interests and politics, yet close no matter the distance in miles...because we love one another and we are all a little wacky! We stay connected by email and refer to each other as the gang. They are as follows:

Kasey Michaels. Leslie Lafoy. Mary McBride. Karen Katz and myself.

Yes, I know, that is only five.

Marcia Evanick was number six. Marcie, as we called her, was warm and kind and compassionate. At our occasional meetings, when she smiled or laughed, we had to smile and laugh with her.

Last July, after a valiant, courageous fight, our beloved Marcie lost the battle of her life to ALS. My she rest in peace.

I will miss you forever, Marce.

Joan

One

Jennifer Dunning had always been indulged and she knew it. How could she not? From the day of her birth she had been pampered and cooed over, not only by her parents but by anyone and everyone who saw her. And yet, as far as she could recall, she had never acted out or thrown temper tantrums when she didn't get her way. She accepted a "no" as final and quietly moved on.

But now she sat on her bed in her room, where she had been hiding for the better part of the past two weeks, searching desperately on her electric-blue laptop for her new life. It was time to leave her parents' home in the exclusive gated community on the outskirts of Dallas. It was time to leave her parents, period.

Jennifer was stunningly beautiful—she had been as a baby, and was even more so at the age of twenty-eight. Tall and willowy with curves in all the right places, she was blessed with long honey-blond hair, dark brown eyes and classic features.

Jennifer was also restless, frustrated and edgy. She had quit her high-paying job as a personal assistant to the CEO of a large company two weeks ago. She was simply sick and tired of listening to the endless daily pep rallies given by her boss—the son of the company owner—who Jennifer considered unfit for the position he held. She was also tired of him eyeing her up and down every time they happened to be in the same room. He was a creep. So, deciding she had had enough, she had resigned.

Jennifer didn't actually need to work. Her parents were wealthy and she was their only child. She also had a large trust fund from her departed fraternal grandmother, and a smaller one from her maternal grandfather, who was still alive. But she liked working. She was intelligent, had a bachelor's degree in science and an MBA, and she enjoyed keeping busy, doing something useful. As a personal assistant, she'd been on her way up the career ladder.

Besides, working was much more interesting than the Dallas social scene. She found the scene boring, as well as pointless. As a youngster she had enjoyed the dancing lessons her mother insisted upon, and she also loved riding, after getting over the initial fear of her horse, which was huge compared to her six-year-old frame. No small ponies for her daughter, her mother had declared. Jennifer would attain her seat while on the back of a full-size Thoroughbred. And she had. Her seat was as elegant by the time she was eleven as that of any expert equestrian.

It was later, as she grew into her late teens, that Jennifer had become tired of the social scene. Lunch with the girls every Wednesday, listening to gossip she couldn't care less about—it had all started to feel so frivolous, and Jennifer had big plans for herself. She'd been preparing to go east, to the University of Pennsylvania and the Wharton School of Business. Her friends all had plans to attend the same college right there in Texas. In short, they were parting ways. But Jennifer decided she'd bear the lunches and the silly talk, as she thought of it, until the end of summer. Then she'd be on her own.

In contrast, her parents had been immersed in the social whirl all her life, unfortunately. It wasn't that they were uncaring—Jennifer knew her parents loved her. It was simply that they weren't there all that much. As a kid, she spent most of her free time with the housekeeper, Ida, who taught her how to clean, or with the cook, Tony, who practically made her a professional chef. As it turned out, Jennifer loved doing hard, honest work with her hands. It filled her with a purpose she hadn't known she'd needed.

After Jennifer finished school, she came back to Dallas and lived in her own apartment with a private entrance in her parents' house. She could have invited anyone she wanted to her place, but she had never had a man stay over. Not that her parents would have minded or objected. She was an adult, after all. It was just that none of the men she knew affected her *that* way.

Maybe because of what had happened during her junior year of high school.

She had never told her parents—or anyone else— about being caught alone on campus by a boy. She'd been leaving school later than most of the students following a meeting with her math teacher. It was January and almost dark, and she was distracted by thoughts of her conversation with the teacher. She wasn't fully alert while weaving through the rows of vehicles in the parking lot as she headed for her car.

The boy was a senior—a clean-cut, all-American star football player. Most of Jennifer's friends had crushes on him. Jennifer didn't, thinking him too cocky and into himself. Perhaps that was the reason he had accosted her that afternoon.

Trapping her between two parked cars, he fumbled with his pants zipper, exposing himself to her. At first, she was too shocked to think. But she came to her senses when he shoved his other hand up her skirt, attempting to yank her panties off.

Frantic, Jennifer had let out an earsplitting scream. Although the parking lot had appeared deserted, a male voice responded with a shouted, "Hey, what the hell?"

Mr. All-American let loose a savage curse, snarling, "You better keep your mouth shut about this, bitch." He sprinted away in the opposite direction.

Without thinking, Jennifer ran to her car, even as she could hear the man who had shouted running toward her. Her parents weren't home when she arrived there, shaken and teary-eyed. Hearing the boy's snarled threat echo in her mind, she had never told anyone of the incident.

Though Jennifer had been physically uninjured, the experience had left her wary of the opposite sex. Over time her anxiety had faded as she realized all males were not like Mr. All-American. She had even indulged her curiosity one time while in college. Although she liked the young man, the act was disappointing, leaving her feeling empty. And so, she had never invited a man to spend the night.

Not that her parents would have noticed even if their

daughter was having a mad, passionate affair. They were busy socializing in Dallas and in the exclusive gated community where they resided, changing partners with their closest friends.

Yes, changing partners.

Jennifer had only recently found out about her parents' game. She hadn't a clue how many friends there had been or how many years they had been experimenting. In truth, she didn't want to know. She could barely look at her parents' faces or be in their company for more than a few minutes. Even though she knew her parents' lifestyle was their business, she felt betrayed, as if they had been lying to her for years about who they really were underneath the façade of "social appropriateness" and their picture-perfect marriage. It made her want to do something to shock them right back.

So she had resigned from her job the day after coming home from work and catching a glimpse of her father and his best friend's wife, Annette Terrell, in a compromising position in one room, and her mother and the woman's husband, William, in a similar position in another.

Now, two weeks later, Jennifer knew she had to leave home, to take a break until the hurt subsided. She could barely look at her parents without feeling ill, and wanting to cry. She loved them, but what she had witnessed had deeply shocked her. Perhaps someday, she would be able to be in the company of her parents without that awful image tormenting her. But that day had not yet arrived.

Alone in her bedroom, Jennifer sat cross-legged on her bed, her laptop balanced on her knees. She was searching for escape, and employment, to keep her mind occupied. In effect, she was intent on running away from home…and her memories. It was time to stop living in a house of lies.

One week later, Jen left her parents a note. It read: *I'm off to see the Wizard—Marsh Grainger, that is, the famously elusive business wizard of Dallas. It's about a new job. I'll be in touch.*

She also emailed her best friends, whom she had met her first year in college. They had remained close ever since, staying in touch mostly by email, phone and texts. Although they all lived within driving distance, they led busy lives—three of the women were married with children, and the other two were busy chasing careers. Even so, "the gang" managed to get together every couple of months.

Hi, all, she wrote them. *I'm taking off for a while, will be in touch soon.*

Jennifer knew the next time she checked her email, there would be long messages from her friends, demanding to know exactly where she was and what she was up to, but she just wasn't ready to talk about what had happened. And she wasn't ready to tell them that she was interviewing with Marshall Grainger, whom they knew had a reputation as a womanizer.

Her mother probably knew, too. She fully expected her mother to start calling her cell phone as soon as she discovered that Jennifer was gone. That was okay— her parents could call all they wanted. It didn't mean she had to answer. After all, even she couldn't entirely explain why Marsh Grainger's ad for an office assistant had appealed to her. But she needed space and distance—and she was pretty sure the wizard, who was rumored to prefer his hill country ranch to the craziness of high society in Dallas, could help her with that.

* * *

Marshall Grainger needed help. He needed an office assistant as well as a cook who would also clean the sprawling Texas hill country home that doubled as his workplace.

A cousin in the wealthy Grainger family of Wyoming, South Dakota and Montana, Marsh was, in a word, loaded. He owned a huge cattle ranch in Colorado, run by an excellent manager and former Marine buddy, Matt Hayes. The ranch had been in Marsh's family for generations. Growing up, he had spent most of his summers there and he knew the ranching business inside and out.

But Marsh was not a cattleman at heart. He was a businessman, considered a force to be reckoned with in more ways than one. He was six foot four inches tall, slim and rangy with rugged features defined by high cheekbones and a strong, square, rock-hard jaw. A thick mane of gleaming hair the exact shade of rich dark chocolate matched the slightly arched brows above slate-gray eyes.

While Marsh owned the building that housed his company, nestled among many other tall buildings in Dallas, he rarely traveled into the city. He avoided the scene in Dallas like the plague, preferring to work at home in the large house set dead center on more than fifty acres.

At present, Marsh was desperately trying not to allow himself to be hopeful. After weeks of using all avenues of advertisements available to him, there was a chance he'd soon be able to hand the ranch books, the household bills and several duties of his main business over to a new assistant.

Someone who was actually qualified had applied for the job. So what if she was a *she?*

Finished paying his current household and ranch bills, he picked up his coffee mug and glanced at his watch as he walked out of the assistant's office, hoping he wouldn't have to spend any time there again in the near future.

It was 1:36 p.m. The appointment with the applicant was at 2. Rinsing his mug, he proceeded to make a fresh pot of coffee. Then again, he mused, after her long drive, the woman might appreciate a cold drink. He checked the fridge; there was cola as well as bottled water. The beer was his. Now all he had to do was wait, which was not Marsh's strong suit. He got busy scouring the sink and wiping down the long countertop.

His former assistant had up and quit on him three months ago, and he hadn't been able to sleep since then—until last night. Just the thought of interviewing someone who was actually qualified and could lighten his load had allowed him to enjoy his first full night's sleep in a long time. Hopefully she would take to the place. At that thought, he grimaced as he sent a quick look around. While tidy, the kitchen needed a thorough cleaning. The same went for the rest of the house. He had done his best to keep up with everything, but the majority of his time was consumed by the myriad details of his businesses. At the end of the day he was only one man.

Marsh had never dreamed finding help would be so hard. After his assistant left, he had received many responses to his ads, but only a few were qualified, and even fewer of those were willing to relocate to "the sticks," as one respondent called it.

The sticks? Marsh had thought with amazement.

Didn't these city dwellers know how popular the hill country was with tourists? Apparently not. They hadn't a clue what they were missing.

But now, hopefully, things would return to normal.

If he could just replace his assistant—and the housekeeper that the man had taken with him to Vegas, to marry—life would be good again.

Marsh thought about what his assistant and the housekeeper had said to him when they'd quit. They had said they were in love.

Love. Yeah. Right.

And if that hadn't been bad enough, the teenage daughter of his nearest neighbor, who had been coming to the house once a week to help the housekeeper, had been ordered to quit. Her parents thought her being alone with him was a bad idea.

Marsh knew precisely what they meant by "bad idea." So he had a reputation with women. So what? He was a healthy male, and the key word was *women*. He was not interested in teenagers. He'd have laughed at the thought if he hadn't been so ticked off.

At the ripe old age of thirty-four, Marsh was bitter and he knew it. He hugged the truth to him like a heating pad, keeping the bitterness alive so he'd never forget.

He had been betrayed—twice. The first time was when he was six years old, by his mother, who had left his father to seek fun in the bright lights, taking a hefty chunk of his father's money with her. Marsh had doubled down on the pain of betrayal at age twenty-four by marrying in a haze of lust only to be told by his young wife that she wasn't about to waste her youth and beauty stuck in the hill country of Texas, popping out babies and ruining her figure. In hindsight, Marsh knew he should have discussed his desire for children before they were married. It would have saved him a lot of trouble and money—especially since he had known deep down inside that he wasn't in love with her. In his estimation, love was an illusion dreamed up by poets and romance writers. But he still would have had children with her, because he truly felt as if he was meant to be a father. He wanted an heir, someone to lavish love on—the only love he truly believed in—who would take over when he was gone.

In some ways, he got lucky. Though his ex took an even larger chunk of his money than his mother had taken of his father's, Marsh gladly wrote the check, happy to get the selfish woman who had clearly married him just for his wealth out of his life and his home.

Then, to top it all off, a couple years later his father had retired, retreating to the ranch where he completed his slow decline toward death, thus also deserting Marsh.

It had been a tough time.

The coffeemaker drew Marsh from his unpleasant reverie with one last gurgle as it finished brewing. Marsh filled his mug and took a careful test sip. The brew was scalding hot but good just the same, even though the carafe, too, needed a thorough washing.

Marsh sighed. As much as he cringed at the very thought of having another female in the house, he hoped this young woman took the job. Jennifer Dunning was her name, and on paper she seemed like a mature, intelligent adult. Her credentials were excellent, almost unbelievably so. Every reference she had listed had come up aces and the investigator's report gave her a clean slate. She was from a wealthy family but apparently enjoyed working. He had even met her prominent parents on one or two occasions but he had never met her. One report he had received said she was not a part of the Dallas social scene, which seemed strange, given her family circumstances.

Basically, he had no idea what to expect.

He had requested an interview at his home. As she was located in Dallas, he was certain she would refuse to travel the considerable distance to his house merely for an interview and that would be the end of it. But she had agreed. Against his better judgment, Marsh set a date and time. Well, today was the day, and it was almost the time…if she showed up.

As a rule, Marsh usually worked in his office until late into the evening hours after dinner. For the past three months, he'd had no choice but to do the work of his assistant and housekeeper as well, which included keeping current on the cattle breeding information and managing the finances for the ranch and the payroll for the men. He barely had time to clean, although he did manage to keep his own bedroom spotless. And forget about cooking—his cooking skills were limited to slapping a sandwich together and heating a can of soup. He did brew a damn good cup of coffee, though.

He shot another look at his watch. Three minutes until two. Carrying his cup, he strolled along the wide slate-covered walkway to the front of the smooth white adobe house. Narrowing his eyes he stared at the black-topped road that turned off the highway to wind its way to the main house. After a long, dry summer, the driveway was coated by a layer of dust.

The beginnings of a frown nudged his eyebrows together as he looked again at his watch. Never late himself, he expected punctuality from others—especially someone applying for employment.

A low beep sounded from a small device attached to his belt. Security was alerting him that someone had driven onto the property. At that moment, he noticed a plume of dust rising from the back of a vehicle moving at a speed that would have made Richard Petty grin. No way was it Jennifer Dunning—he'd never met a woman who drove like that in all his life. It was Matt, or a special delivery, which was probably for the best anyway.

Marsh slashed another glance at his watch. It was exactly two when the old white Cadillac came to a screeching stop directly in front of the flagstone entranceway. The driver's-side door was thrown open and a woman stepped out, slamming the door behind her.

Oh, hell.

She was absolutely gorgeous. A bit above average height, maybe five-eight or so, she had a long mass of honey-blond hair, dark brown eyes, a lovely face with well-defined features, a lush mouth and a curvaceous body. She was basically a man's fantasy come to life.

Dammit, Marsh thought as every muscle in his body grew taut. Jennifer Dunning was the last thing he needed within a hundred miles, let alone inside his home. It had been over two weeks since he had forced himself to leave the ranch and go to his office in Dallas…and as long since he'd been with a woman. How was he going to manage this?

"Mr. Grainger?" Her voice was both cool and seductive. She extended a slim-fingered hand and smiled, revealing perfect white teeth. What else? "I'm Jennifer Dunning."

I was afraid you'd say that. Marsh kept the thought to himself and offered a faint smile in return. He took her hand, surprised by her strong grip.

Something too close to awareness caused an itch in

his palm. He released her hand and gestured for her to precede him along the walkway.

"This will lead to the kitchen," he said, trying to ignore the enticing movement of her rounded hips as she walked ahead of him. "I thought you might like something to drink after your long drive. We can talk there."

"That's fine with me. I'd love a cup of coffee." She turned to offer him another one of those heart-stopping smiles that set off every alarm bell in Marsh's head.

The interview didn't last long. Her intelligent answers exceeded his expectations. Marsh hired her before she had finished her coffee. He was immediately sorry he'd done so, but dammit, he needed the help. He was a grown man—he could keep things under control.

Couldn't he?

Jennifer Dunning was walking, talking temptation. And Marsh certainly wasn't immune to women. Every man needed R & R now and then. But he was confident he could handle the situation—and her. Hell, they'd be in two separate offices located in two separate rooms.

He sighed. He'd be fine…if she turned out to be a nice, quiet assistant who did her job and stayed out of his way.

A woman who drives like that? Not a chance. "So, when can you start?" he asked, holding out hope she would say as soon as next week.

As if she hadn't heard, Jennifer glanced around the room. "Have you found someone for the housekeeping position?"

Marsh frowned. "No, why do you ask? Does the place look that messy?"

She smiled. "Not at all. The ad online mentioned living quarters for the housekeeper attached to the house."

He nodded, curious. What was she getting at? "Yes... why?"

She didn't hesitate. "I can start tomorrow, if I can move into those quarters until you hire a housekeeper. I have my stuff in my car."

Dead silence, for a moment. "You brought all your things with you on the basis of an interview?" Marsh asked. "What if I hadn't hired you?"

Jennifer shrugged. "I'd have found something else, somewhere else. I'm not in a hurry. But no, I didn't bring *all* my things." She flashed a brilliant smile at him, and this one Marsh felt from his hairline to his... never mind. "I would have needed an 18-wheeler for that."

Uh-huh, he thought, aching in all the wrong places and wondering if he had just made the biggest mistake of his life. "Miss Dunning, are you certain you want this job?"

"Jen," she said.

"What?"

"I prefer Jen," she answered. "And yes, I am certain. I wouldn't have bothered interviewing if I didn't want it." She gave him a strange look. "Why, have you changed your mind?"

"No." Marsh gave a quick shake of his head, ignoring the voice inside himself that was telling him to take the out she'd just offered. "I haven't changed my mind...Jen."

"Okay, then can I use the housekeeper's living quarters temporarily?"

"Yeah, sure, why not," he said. "Considering the kind of responses I've had, it might be a while."

She frowned. "Exactly what kind of responses have you received?"

He shrugged. "Oh, things like, 'it's too isolated,' 'too far from Dallas or any other decent-size city,' and on and on."

"Too isolated?" Jen repeated in a tone of disbelief. "There are a lot of towns in this area. From what I gather, the entire hill country is overrun with tourists." She paused, and seemed to size him up for a moment, as if suddenly questioning the wisdom of what she'd just done. "That was one of the reasons I asked if I could have the housekeeper's quarters. I wasn't certain I could find accommodations anywhere close by."

Marsh ignored the way she was looking at him. "Well, glad to be of help," he said, as neutrally as possible.

She relaxed and flashed that smile. "I think the location is perfect."

Marsh felt as if a cool finger had just trailed his spine. Ignoring it, he said the first thing that jumped into his rattled mind.

"Would you like to look at the apartment now?"

"Yes, please." Finishing off her coffee, she stood and started for the door. "I'll go get my stuff."

"I'll help you," Marsh said. "Drive your car around to the garages at the side. There's a private entrance to the apartment there."

To Marsh's surprise, Jen didn't have all that much. He had expected to find her car packed solid with all the "necessities" most of the women he knew needed for a week away. But Jen had two suitcases, a canvas carry-on bag, a computer case and a midsize carton, which drew a mild grunt from him when he hoisted it from the trunk.

"Books," she said, smiling at him.

"No kidding," Marsh said, sliding the heavy carton

under one arm. "And I was just about to tell you how light you were traveling."

"A girl's got to have her books," Jen said as she headed off in the direction he indicated, giving him a luscious view that made him sure he was going to regret the day Jennifer Dunning came into his life.

As they walked through the garage to the apartment, Jen took note of the four very expensive cars parked in each bay and the workhorse truck in the fifth one. The cars—and the garage itself—were cleaner than the interior of the house. Jen smiled to herself as Marsh crossed the spotless cement floor to a side door.

"Will you get the door, please? It's unlocked."

"Of course," she said, skirting around him to open it and stepping back for him to precede her. Nodding in thanks, he started up a flight of stairs. To her surprise, the stairway led into a long hallway inside the house, not above the garage, as she had assumed. So, the quarters weren't attached to the house, they were *inside* the house.

Mmm, she mused, *maybe this wasn't such a good idea after all.* That thought was immediately followed by, *Oh, grow up, Jennifer, surely Mr. Grainger wouldn't try anything with his assistant, would he?* At the thought, Jen felt a strange twinge in the pit of her stomach that wasn't altogether unpleasant.

She ignored the sensation and decided she was being ridiculous. The door would have a lock...or so she hoped.

Dropping the suitcase, Marsh dug a ring of keys from his pocket and removed one, unlocking and opening the door. "After you," he said, standing back to let her pass.

"Thank you." Jen entered, pleasantly surprised by the cozy living room. She heard him sigh behind her.

"I'm sorry," he said, following her into the room. "The place needs a good cleaning. If I'd have known…"

"It's fine," she said, cutting him off. "I'll take care of it."

"Possibly I could get the young woman who used to help out once a week before the housekeeper…"

"It's all right. Really." She smiled. "I learned how to clean from the best." Jen was on the move as she spoke, checking out the bedroom, the bathroom, the small dining area and lastly the kitchen. He trailed behind her.

Making a quick turn, she almost crashed into him.

"Sorry." They spoke in unison.

Jen laughed.

Marsh smiled. "So, what do you think?"

"I like it," she said. "This kitchen is fabulous."

"You can cook?"

She swung a wicked grin at him. "I'm a damn good cook. I practically grew up with the chef in my mother's kitchen."

"Uh-huh." He hesitated before saying, "I'm a disaster in the kitchen. The last decent meal I had was in a restaurant two weeks ago."

"Too bad," she commiserated with him. "I love to cook."

"Wanna get paid for it?"

Jen frowned. "What do you mean?"

"I'll up your salary by half if you'll take over the cooking in the main kitchen downstairs."

Jen extended her hand to him. "You've got yourself a cook." Her palm tingled at the touch of his rough, callused skin against hers. It wasn't the first time—she had felt the same sensation when they had shaken hands before, only then she had put it down to nervousness over the interview. Then there was that funny twist in her midsection a short time ago.

She didn't know what it all was exactly, but she didn't like it.

Fortunately, the contact lasted only a moment. He released her hand and moved to the door, pausing again to glance back at her.

"You don't have to start your administrative duties tomorrow, as you offered. Take the next three days to get set up in here. I'll be in my office. If you need any-thing—" he nodded at the slim phone on the countertop "—just hit number one. Any questions?"

"Yes," Jen said. "Since I assume there is no food here, where is the nearest grocery store?"

He frowned.

Jen had the distinct impression he frowned a lot.

"I thought you were going to cook in the kitchen downstairs."

Men. Squashing an urge to roll her eyes, Jen made do with a silent sigh. "I will need a few things in here, as well. You know, coffee, milk, other staples." Straight-faced, she admitted, "I'm a night snacker."

A shade of a smile crossed his lips. Jen had another distinct impression: that he didn't smile all that often. Shame. It was quite an attractive smile.

"Look, leave the grocery shopping until tomorrow. There is stuff in the downstairs kitchen—in the pan-try, fridge and freezer. If you'll come along now, you can take things for tonight and make a shopping list for tomorrow."

"Okay." Jen followed him from the room. Getting to the kitchen was simple. They walked to the end of the hallway to a large landing, where a broad open staircase curved down to an equally broad foyer at the front of the house.

At the bottom of the stairs, Marsh turned left and strode along another hallway that led to the kitchen at the back of the house. By Jen's calculations, her new living quarters were directly above the kitchen and formal dining room. From the dining room's sliding glass doors, she caught a glimpse of a large patio and a swimming pool.

Gorgeous property, nicer than the too-formal look of her parents' home, she was thinking. *What will it feel like to live in a place like this as the hired help?*

"Okay, the kitchen's all yours," Marsh said. "I've got work to do."

"Wait," Jen said.

He frowned again but this time, impatience flashed across his features, making them look severe. Slowly, he raised one eyebrow.

If he meant to intimidate, he succeeded.

But Jen was not about to let him know it. "Jot down a few of your food preferences," she said, fully aware that her request sounded like an order. "Meanwhile, I'll start a list of the things we'll need." She raised an eyebrow right back at him. "Okay?"

He sighed, gave her a terse nod and left the room.

When he was gone, Jen exhaled. Working for Marshall Grainger was going to be a challenge, in a number of ways, not the least of which was remaining professional and not losing her temper right along with him.

Finding a notebook and pencils in a drawer, she began opening cabinets. None of them contained foodstuffs; a few were completely empty. Then she discovered the double pantry next to the fridge. Now she was getting somewhere. There were plenty of dried foods:

flour, sugar, cereals and canned goods, except for soup. There were only two cans in an otherwise empty area.

She stared at the shelf for a moment, wondering whether her new employer didn't like soup, or loved it so much it was a regular for him.

Recalling his words, she shook her head. He had admitted to being a lousy cook. Conclusion? The man had been practically living on soup. After checking out the fridge, she added sandwiches to the list of things he'd been living on. Other than two slices of cheese wrapped in plastic, a nearly empty carton of eggs, a small package of bacon, a half-empty carton of milk and a couple of slices of bread, along with some beer and soda, the fridge was empty.

Jen opened the freezer door on the side-by-side. Now, this looked better. The freezer was packed and everything was dated. Maybe there was hope for Marsh Grainger after all, she thought with a smile.

Her shopping list completed, she sent a slow look around the room. The countertop looked spotless, as if very recently cleaned. Hmm, she mused. Had her boss given it a quick cleaning before she arrived?

Had he done that for her benefit?

Giving herself a mental get-with-it shake, she glanced at the clock.

It was eight minutes after three. Jen figured she had time enough to clean the kitchen. But first, dinner. She rummaged around in the freezer and grabbed a package of ground turkey and a bag of mixed veggies with an herb sauce. Within minutes she had a turkey stew cooking in the slow cooker on the counter.

Turkey stew would have to do. Smiling at her silly rhyme, she pulled out some cleaning supplies, slipped on a pair of plastic gloves and got down to the business at hand.

A couple hours later, her skin moist with perspiration from her efforts, Jen stood in the kitchen doorway admiring the results. The room was spotless. A sense of satisfaction brought a small smile to her lips—Ida would be proud.

After touching the floor tiles to see if they were dry, Jen walked to the phone and hit the 1 button.

"What is it, Ms. Dunning?"

Jen didn't miss the exasperated note in Marshall's voice. Keeping her own voice carefree and chipper, she said, "Dinner is ready whenever you are." She paused, then deliberately added, "sir."

"Thank you. But don't call me that."

His tone had lightened a bit. Jen smirked. "You're welcome."

"I'll be there in a little while."

"Take your time, it will keep. I'm going up to my place now."

"What about you?"

She couldn't quite read his meaning. Was he worried she wanted to dine with him? Or did he want her to? "I've eaten, thank you. What time would you like breakfast?"

"Is six-thirty okay with you?"

Good grief, was he actually asking her instead of telling her? "Yes," she briskly answered, "six-thirty will be fine." She waited a heartbeat before saying, "Good night, *sir*."

Without giving him a chance to respond, Jen hit the off button, leaving the room with a jaunty step.

Two

Jen sat in a comfortable chair, sipping hot coffee while gazing around the living room in her new quarters. Though not very large, the room was cozy and would be even better with a bit of decorating.

She'd get at the cleaning tomorrow. Since she had the next three days off, she could take her time, she thought. But as she tried to make a mental list of everything she wanted to do, her mind kept drifting…to her new employer.

What was his deal, anyway? She mused, hearing an echo of his hard voice, seeing again the sharpness of his steel-gray eyes.

Tough man, Marshall Grainger. Though she had never seen him in person before, Jen had seen him in the paper and had heard about him. And there was plenty to hear—good and bad, but never indifferent.

He had married young, and divorced soon after—

a sticky affair from what Jen had heard. She gathered that the young woman, a genuine beauty, had expected Marsh to introduce her into the highest social circles in Texas. But apparently Mr. Marshall Grainger wasn't into the social scene, and never had been. So, goodbye wife—and goodbye to a large slice from his money pie.

But, rumor had it, his mother had done the same deal to his father, and Marsh was one bitter man. He disdained women, while not above using them for his own convenience.

Luckily for her she was only here to work. She had no interest in Marsh Grainger, and she intended to keep it that way. So what if he was as handsome as the day was long? Jen had never had a problem keeping her cool around good-looking men—she wasn't about to start now.

She rose from the comfy chair and walked to the kitchen to rinse her cup. It was time to put clean sheets on the bed, have a shower and hit the sack. *Breakfast for my steely-eyed boss at six-thirty,* she reminded herself.

Jen had a full breakfast of bacon, eggs, hash browns, toast and fresh coffee ready when Marsh strode into the kitchen at precisely six-thirty the next morning. Unlike most CEOs going to work, he was dressed in faded jeans, a chambray shirt and well-worn running shoes.

He looked terrific.

"Good morning," she greeted him cheerily, dishing up the meal onto two plates.

"Urmph," he responded as he seated himself at the solid-oak table.

Jen stifled a smile and placed his breakfast in front of him, then put her plate on a tray and started to head upstairs.

"Where are you going?" he asked, his forkful of eggs in midair between his plate and his mouth.

Gritting her teeth at his imperious tone, while reminding herself that this grouchy man was her employer, Jen managed to dredge up a pleasant reply. "I'm going upstairs."

He motioned at the chair opposite. "Have a seat. There are a few things I want to go over with you."

Offloading her food from the tray to the table, Jen sat and patiently watched him enjoying her culinary efforts.

"Eat," he said, snapping off a bite of crisp bacon with his strong white teeth. "We can talk over coffee."

They ate the meal in dead silence. Jen was tempted to speak, but she squashed the urge, determined to make him start the conversation.

As soon as he sat back and laid his napkin beside his plate, Jen was on her feet, clearing. Deliberately making him wait, she stashed the dishes in the dishwasher before pouring the coffee and then sitting down again. Wrapping her hands around the mug, she looked directly into his eyes, and was startled to find herself fascinated by the odd silvery color. She again felt that funny tingling sensation inside, deep inside, and again she didn't like it. The feeling was too…too out of her control. She quickly looked away.

"I'll be leaving later this morning," he said. "I have a few business appointments. You'll have the place to yourself for the entire weekend as I won't be back until Monday."

A strange relief washed through her at the thought that she wouldn't have to see Marsh for a few days. It was mixed with a sense of disappointment that she chose to ignore. "Great," she said. "It'll give me plenty of time to get settled in."

"You have no reason to be concerned about being alone here. I have—"

Jen frowned, interrupting. "Actually, I like being alone."

Marsh leveled a cool look at her; apparently he didn't appreciate being interrupted. "Any woman should be afraid of being alone on a property this size," he growled. "I'm a wealthy man. That, plus the size of the place, makes it a target. In addition to a man who takes care of the horses, I have security all over the grounds."

"I didn't notice any security when I drove up," she said, taking a sip of the coffee.

He gave her a wry look. "That's the idea—you're not supposed to notice them. But trust me, they were there, and I was notified of your arrival."

"You have horses?" she asked, ignoring his tone.

"Yes, I have horses."

When he didn't add anything further, she asked, "What about the office work?"

"That can wait until Monday. I brought everything up to date before you arrived." He lifted a hand to a breast pocket and withdrew a white bank envelope and a small black leather case. "That should be enough cash to purchase whatever you need," he said. "The case is an alarm. If you hear or see anything that doesn't seem right to you, press the button. There will be security here in minutes. It will also open the garage. I'm going to pull the truck out so you can park your car."

Sighing, she reluctantly took the case.

He frowned at her. "Keep it with you at all times. And that's an order."

"Yes, sir."

His eyes narrowed. "Oh, and I also listed a few of

my favorite meals…as you asked," he added in a dry-as-dust tone.

"Thank you." Jen pushed back her chair and stood. "If you'll excuse me now, I'm going up to clean the apartment…unless you have other instructions for me?" She raised her brows.

He nodded his head, also standing. "There is one more thing." He sent a slow glance around the room. "You did a good job on the kitchen. It's spotless."

A tiny smile played at the corners of her mouth. "Not quite," she said. "The curtains need laundering."

For a moment Marsh simply stared at her, then, with a shake of his head, he started for the hallway. "I'll see you sometime Monday." With that he strode from the room.

Jen watched him go, wondering just what kind of power struggle she had gotten herself into with Marsh Grainger.

She spent the rest of the day giving the apartment a thorough cleaning. By the time she looked up, it was time for supper. Yet as busy as she was, there were moments—too many, to Jen's way of thinking—when thoughts of Marsh pushed past her guard to tease her imagination.

Jen didn't appreciate his intrusion. He was her employer. Period. Nothing more. Who was he, really, other than a tough and bitter man? In all truth, he had a right to his bitterness, but it was none of her concern.

Still, the thoughts persisted. Why? In a word, Marshall Grainger was all male. A ruggedly handsome, sexy-as-hell male at that.

Startled by her last thought, Jen gave herself a mental shake. *Get it together, woman,* she told herself. *Marsh may be all those things, but he uses women, and you don't want any part of that.*

Forget him and get back to work.

When she had finished cleaning, Jen took a long, soothing shower, slipped into a nightshirt, then sat down with her laptop to contact her friends. Naturally there were emails from every one of them, demanding more information. She sent them a group email back, saying she had gotten a new job and would get back to them later, after she had settled into the position and had more complete information to offer.

The fact of the matter was, Jen was not quite ready to tell her friends what had happened to send her running from her home. Nor was she ready to tell them that she was living under Marsh Grainger's roof. Tired, muscles aching from the unusual flurry of physical activity, Jen was then content to drop into bed early. With any luck, she'd fall asleep quickly before she had time for more thoughts of Marshall Grainger.

Saturday morning Jen woke refreshed if still a bit achy, proof of the fact that she had been idle too long. She had stayed in shape playing tennis and horseback riding whenever she could, but while musing on her future options during the past several weeks she had barely left her apartment. The cleaning exercise had done her good.

She dressed in designer jeans, a pin-tucked white shirt and flat-heeled boots. Deciding to grab breakfast in town, she left the house for her shopping spree.

She looked inside the envelope Marsh had given her. Along with the short list of his favorite meals and directions to the nearest mall, Marsh had left her a ridiculous amount of money. Jen rolled her eyes but couldn't stop the smile that spread across her face.

Either Marsh Grainger had no idea what things actually cost, or he was an extremely generous man underneath that gruff exterior.

It was a lovely, warm autumn day, perfect for shopping. As she headed down the driveway, Jen kept an eye out for signs of the security he had told her about. She didn't see hide nor hair until she neared the stone pillars flanking the entranceway. A short distance off the road, barely visible, an all-terrain vehicle was parked next to a low hanging tree. As she drove through the entranceway, she thrust her arm out the window and waved as she hit the horn. She laughed as she received a wave and toot in return.

Well, at least the security is friendly, Jen thought, applying a little pressure to the gas pedal. She drove first to the mall Marsh had mentioned, and went into the first shop she came to displaying home decorations.

Not into knick-knacks, Jen chose three pictures in three different sizes. The smaller pictures she chose were pastoral scenes, one of a field covered with Texas bluebonnets, the other of a basket of wildflowers set on one end of a long library table. But the largest one, for the living room, was a rendering in black-and-white of a ship, alone on a wide sea. For some reason, it reminded her of Marsh, alone in that big, remote house.

The thought sent a little shiver through her. *Now, that's simply ridiculous,* she chided herself, trying and failing to ignore the feeling. *There's no reason to be thinking of Marsh as a lonely man—in fact, that's just plain dangerous.* Pushing away her thoughts, Jen left the mall and headed for the supermarket.

The sun was beginning to set as Jen drove back onto

the property. Her glance automatically shifted to the tree. There was a vehicle there, but a different one. Again she hit the horn and waved, and again she was greeted in kind.

In high spirits, satisfied with her selection of decorations for the apartment, Jen unloaded the car and set to work stashing the food in cabinets, fridge and freezer. As she worked, a curiosity set in about the rest of the house—and, if she was honest with herself, Marsh. It wouldn't exactly be snooping, she decided. Just… investigating. After all, she'd be working here—she might as well familiarize herself with the place. She quietly slipped into the main part of the house and found herself peeking into six bedrooms and five bathrooms, all of which were long past due for a good dusting and vacuuming. Stepping into the last room at the end of the hallway, Jen felt her breath catch when she opened the door to the huge room that obviously belonged to Marsh.

The room was the complete opposite of opulent—it was Spartan, and it was spotless, not a speck of dust anywhere. A tiny smile feathered her lips. It seemed Mr. Marshall Grainger liked a clean room just as much as she did.

The furniture was plain, straight lines, solid oak. The bed—his bed—was enormous. His color scheme consisted primarily of black, white and red, stark but effective, somehow perfect for him.

Feeling more like a snoop by the minute but unable to resist, Jen moved into the room, going to the row of sliding mirrored closet doors along one wall. One entire section was full of tailored suits, one of them a tuxedo. Another section held nothing but dress shirts in every color imaginable, including white with black stripes. She liked that one, imagining how sexy he'd look in it.

Sexy? she thought. *What am I doing in here?*

But Jen kept going—she couldn't seem to make herself stop. There was something too enticing about being this close to Marsh. The next section held jeans, some faded, some brand-new. They were the longest jeans she'd ever seen in her life, perfect for a tall drink of water like Marsh. The last section held casual shirts of every style and hue. On the floor beneath each area were shoes—dress shoes, work boots, riding boots, running shoes. Jen laughed. And she thought she was a shoe maniac!

Closing the sliding doors, she opened another door in the bedroom to find a good-size dressing room and a spacious bathroom. The bathtub was huge, with water jets set into the sides. A compact shower stall sat next to the tub. The black-and-white marble vanity top looked much like the surface of his dresser—sparse and neat. A toothbrush was set in a marble brush holder, and a woven metal basket contained a hairbrush, and several unopened bars of soap. Spartan indeed, she thought, slowly stepping back into the hallway.

She ignored the little twinge of guilt she felt about her "investigation," thinking that in the short time she was in his room, she had learned much about him.

Marshall Grainger was wealthy beyond belief—that was a given. He was also a man who lived life stripped to the bone, despite all the clothing. His bathroom vanity held nothing but the bare essentials, including what Jen knew was a very expensive bottle of cologne. She hadn't smelled it on him so far. She wondered if he'd been wearing it when he'd left for Houston. Perhaps he didn't have any meetings or appointments to attend— maybe there was a woman there, waiting for him.

The very idea caused a strange twist in Jen's chest, a twist that felt like jealousy. *What would the woman be like? Beautiful? Of course. Sophisticated? Naturally.* The strange jealousy she felt grew stronger. *Was this woman his lover?*

Bringing herself up abruptly, Jen quickly turned and went roaming through the rest of the house. It was absolutely gorgeous. Open rooms, one flowing into another. She stepped into one and somehow knew she had entered her office. It was roomy yet utilitarian, containing everything she would need. It even had two club chairs, one in front of the large desk, the other to one side. She liked it at once.

Exiting that room, Jen went to the next one: Marsh's office. It was locked.

Walking back toward her apartment, Jen contemplated the situation. The beautiful house needed some care. She hadn't been hired to clean, but damn, such a house should shine.

She sighed. She had all day tomorrow to herself with nothing pressing to do. A smile touched her lips as she made a decision. Tomorrow, she would clean the big house, just to see if the boss noticed anything different.

Of course, Jen assured herself as she mounted the stairs to her apartment, her decision had nothing to do with pleasing him. Why should it? She had nothing to prove but her ability as his assistant. It didn't matter what Marshall Grainger thought of her.

Did it?

She suddenly imagined herself back in Marsh's bedroom, tidying it up, making it perfect for his return. When she remembered that his room was already spot-

less and that there was no need for her to go back in
there, she blushed, hot and fierce, and promised to push
all thoughts of Marsh from her mind for the rest of the
night.

Marsh sat across the table from the beautiful woman
his business acquaintance had introduced him to mere
hours ago. Admittedly, Marsh was on the prowl, itch-
ier than usual for a woman. Without a twinge of conscience, he had invited the woman—Chandra was her
name—to have dinner with him that evening. But now,
after several hours, her appeal had faded, through no
real fault of her own. She couldn't help it if she wasn't
Miss Jennifer Dunning.

When Chandra looked at him expectantly, he realized she was waiting for some kind of response. He
hadn't a clue what she was talking about; he hadn't exactly been paying attention. He took a chance and nodded, and that appeared to satisfy her.

Being inattentive, his conscience kicked into action.
What in hell am I doing here?

Marsh knew the answer—he simply didn't want to
look at it too closely. He had been hoping for a bed
partner later in the evening, and Chandra had seemed
a good choice. Now all he wanted was a bed to himself.

That wasn't quite true, either.

In truth, he ached for one woman: Jennifer Dunning.

He had been in her company…how long? Not much
more than an hour or so, total? It was ridiculous. Plus,
she was now an employee, and he never fooled around
with employees. Of course, other than the previous
housekeeper, who was pushing fifty, he had never had
an employee living in his home, either. What was it
about her that got to him so strongly?

"…and I told him he could just go to hell."

Marsh blinked himself back into the moment. "You did?" he asked, because Chandra had paused again and he knew he had to say something.

"Certainly," Chandra declared. "The man insulted me by assuming I'd go to bed with him a few hours after meeting him."

Marsh gave her a wry smile. "Yes, of course," he agreed. "I don't blame you in the least." He almost added "the cad" but thought that might be a bit over the top.

"Ah, here's dinner now," she said, satisfaction curving her lips as the server placed their meals before them.

After dinner, Marsh drove Chandra straight home to her condo on the outskirts of the city. "You don't need to get out," she said, even though he hadn't made a move to do so. "It's perfectly safe."

"Yes, I see the doorman," he said, eyeing the burly uniformed man standing sentinel by the entrance.

"Thank you for a lovely dinner," she said, as the doorman strolled forward to open the door for her.

"Thank you for joining me," he answered, hoping his tone didn't reveal his relief. He politely added, "I'm glad you were free for the evening."

"And I." She smiled with a tinge of disappointment, and slid from the seat.

Marsh never liked disappointing a lady—even one who seemed to have given him a line about not going to bed with a man hours after meeting him—but his mind was clearly elsewhere this evening. He'd put the Jag he kept in Houston into Drive before she'd reached the doorway, and Jen was back on his mind by the time he pulled into traffic.

Why the hell had he hired her?

Marsh sighed. He had hired Jen because he was getting desperate. She was intelligent, personable, fully qualified, friendly and willing to do the cooking.

Yet, he had to admit, she was the reason he had come to Houston. After meeting her, when the touch of her hand made his palm—and parts south—itch, and when that itch had swiftly turned into a familiar warmth that spread through his body, he knew he was in trouble.

He wanted her. He had wanted her within minutes of meeting her, and it had played hell with his normally sound judgment. So, afraid he'd do or say something unacceptable, he manufactured a business trip to put some distance between them, calling his friend Scott to set up a meeting in Houston. To his confused embarrassment, after sitting across the breakfast table from Jen that morning, he couldn't get to the airstrip soon enough. He had arrived forty-five minutes earlier than he had asked his pilot to be there.

Marsh kept the plane primarily to get from his house in Dallas to the ranch in Colorado in a hurry if he needed to, but used it himself for quick trips like this one. Except that this trip had been unnecessary. He felt like an idiot, getting all hot and sweaty over a woman he had just met. Sure he had been all hot and sweaty over women before, like his previous wife, but he had been a lot younger then. And look where that had gotten him.

Well, the heat was gone now and so was the sweat. Marsh was resolved to revert to form—cool and aloof. He just had to remember that Jen was an employee, nothing more.

Cool and aloof, that would be his mantra.

Marsh could only hope.

* * *

Satisfyingly tired from the day spent cleaning the house, Jen lay curled up in bed, floating in the in-between world of wakefulness and sleep.

The growling sound of a vehicle jerked her awake. She glanced at the clock on the nightstand—it read 1:30 a.m. She heard the automatic garage door open, then slide shut again. Moments later she heard the kitchen door. She rolled onto her back, listening.

Although she would never have admitted it, Jen had not slept easily the previous two nights. She had wakened often, listening. She told herself it was just her new surroundings, that she wasn't used to sleeping in the quiet hill country yet.

Yeah. Right.

A sigh whispered through her lips. Her eyelids grew heavy, slowly closing. *Marsh was home.* Too fuzzy-minded to question the comfort she drew from that thought, Jen drifted into a deep, restful sleep within seconds.

She woke the next morning feeling rested, and had breakfast ready when Marsh entered the kitchen at precisely six-thirty. She had wondered if he would make it after returning to the house so late, but there he was, wide-awake, alert and handsome as the rugged devil.

"Good morning." She greeted him with a smile and a large plate in hand. He did not return her smile.

"Morning," he said as he sat down and drew his napkin over his jean-clad knees. "Smells good."

"Thanks," she said, setting the plate of eggs, potatoes and a large steak in front of him. She turned back to the counter to get her own plate.

"Have a seat." It wasn't so much an invitation as an order.

But today, Jen didn't mind. He was the boss, after all. They ate in silence again. Marsh didn't say a word until after she had removed the plates and served the coffee.

"You cleaned the house." His tone was hard.

"Yes." She held his gaze, slowly arching one questioning brow.

"Why?"

Her other brow went up in surprise. "Because it needed cleaning."

"Yes, it did. But you weren't hired to clean."

"I cleaned the kitchen," Jen shot back at him. "You didn't object to that."

"I hired you to cook," he said, returning fire. "So of course I wouldn't object to you cleaning the kitchen. That has nothing to do with the rest of the house." He frowned, perplexed. "I don't get it. Why would a woman like you even consider cooking and cleaning in any house?"

"What do you mean, a woman like me?"

"You're from a rich family, dammit. And I didn't mean 'a woman like you' as a slur, if that's what you're thinking. You don't need to work at all, never mind cook and clean. It doesn't make sense."

Jen sighed, fully aware she should have expected this reaction from him. Before she could begin to explain, he tossed more at her.

"You come from a well-known, wealthy family, grew up in the lap of luxury in the highest social circles—"

"Hold it right there." Jen cut him off. She shoved her chair back, scraping it over the floor tiles as she slapped her hands on her hips. He opened his mouth. "First and foremost, Mr. Grainger, I am not a member of any social circle. I am not a social butterfly. My parents are the socialites. I was practically raised by my parents' housekeeper and chef, Ida and Tony."

She paused for breath but rushed on before he could get a word out.

"They gave me a sense of being loved for myself, and taught me the value of honest work. Ida taught me how to take care of a beautiful house. Tony taught me how to prepare delicious meals. *This* is a beautiful house," she continued. "It deserves to be kept that way. And yes, I'm used to well-prepared meals."

Marsh was quiet for a moment, as if waiting to see if she was finished. When she didn't speak, he said, "It will only get dusty again."

She rolled her eyes. "Then I'll clean it again."

"And what about the work you were hired to do?"

Jen made a quick study of his closed expression, trying to decide if he was about to fire her from a job she hadn't yet begun. At any other time in her life, she wouldn't have cared. Now, for some strange reason she didn't want to examine too closely, she *did* care. She wanted this job, cleaning and all.

She wanted to stay here with him.

"I'll clean on Saturdays." She again arched one brow. "Or were you thinking to have me work in the office on weekends, too?"

"No, of course not." He heaved a sigh. "I'll pay you for the cleaning."

"Thank you." She smiled at her victory. "I'll get the breakfast things away so I can get started in the office." To her surprise, he began clearing the table.

"I'll help here," he said, carrying dishes to the dishwasher. "The sooner we can get started, the better. I have a lot of work to do." His voice was rough, as if

he were embarrassed about helping with anything do-
mestic.

Jen fought against a laugh. "Yes, sir."

He sighed again. "I asked you not to call me 'sir'."

She nodded. "I know."

She was really beginning to enjoy being with him.
Was she nuts? He had barely been civil to her since
she'd arrived at the house. How could she even think
she was beginning to like the man?

Maybe she had been fawned over for too long, by
her parents, and Ida and Tony.

Possibly, a man like Marshall Grainger was just what
she needed. A no-nonsense, straight-talking man with
a perfect smile and silver eyes.

No doubt about it, she thought. *I am nuts.*

Three

Marsh sat in front of the computer, a newer model than the one Jen had used at her previous job. She told him the machine was new to her, so he began with the basics. He had drawn another chair up to the desk next to him. They were so close that whenever he turned to explain something to her, or she leaned in to get a closer look at the data on the screen, their thighs briefly brushed against each other.

It was purely accidental and yet Jen felt a quiver of awareness when his hard thigh touched her soft one.

He smelled good, and not of the cologne she'd seen in his bedroom. Jen wished she had noticed the smell of his woodsy soap and his natural musky male scent earlier while they'd cleared away the breakfast things, so she could have been prepared. Now, here, sitting so close to him, his scent enveloped her. And it wasn't a bad thing—not at all.

Yanking her mind away from Marsh and back to the business at hand, she reached across him with her right arm to point at data on the screen she didn't understand. At the same time, he lifted his hand, his forearm brushing over her breast.

For an instant they both froze. She pulled her arm back, he dropped his hand. Jen tingled all the way down to her toenails.

"I—" he began.

"It's all right." She cut him off, her voice as cool and calm as she could manage. "I know it wasn't deliberate."

"That's right, it wasn't, but still—"

Again she interrupted him. "Let's just get back to work. Okay?"

"Yeah, sure," he agreed, his tone rough-edged. "What was your question?"

Instead of reaching across him, she read the part she wasn't sure of. The tension quivering between them still hovered as he explained.

They broke for lunch not much later. "I'm going to my office," he said, starting for the room opposite hers. "I'll be with you in a few minutes."

"I'll start lunch," she said. "Is a chef salad okay with you?"

His office door shut before he could give her an answer.

Jen went into the kitchen, threw the salad together and stood at the counter eating while getting the ingredients together for Yankee pot roast for dinner. She was peeling potatoes—trying to ignore the fact that her body was still tingling from Marsh's touch—when he entered.

"Aren't you going to sit down?" he asked, digging into his salad.

"I'm about finished," Jen answered, popping the last

forkful into her mouth as she slid the roast pan into the oven. The last thing she needed right now was to sit close to Marsh Grainger one second sooner than she had to.

They were back at her desk fifteen minutes later, both making sure to keep as much distance between them as possible. By midafternoon, Jen was up to speed.

"I think I can handle it now myself," she said, aware that his scent was making her overwarm.

Marsh nodded. He pushed back the chair and glanced at his watch. "You can quit for the day, you've got a lot of data to mentally process. I'll see you at dinner."

"Is six all right?"

"That'll be fine." His office door shut, but Jen stayed right where she was, needing a moment to gather herself together.

Working with Marsh Grainger was definitely going to be difficult if she couldn't even handle accidental physical contact with the man.

Some employee *she* was going to be.

That night, Jen's cell phone rang. She wasn't surprised to see that it was her mother calling, wondering what had taken her so long. Jen sighed as she answered. "Hello, Mother."

"Hello, Mother? *Hello, Mother?*" Celia Dunning came close to shouting, and Celia rarely shouted at anything. "You take off leaving only a note saying 'I'm off to see the wizard,' and all you say is 'Hello, Mother'?"

"What else am I supposed to say?" Jen answered, gritting her teeth to hold her temper. "I left you a note. You couldn't have been too perturbed—it's been almost a week since I left." Try as she might, Jen couldn't ignore the hurt she felt over the fact that it had taken her mother so long to call.

"I'm sorry." Celia now sounded contrite. "Your father decided on the spur of the moment Thursday evening that he felt lucky and wanted to fly to Las Vegas. He was right," she went on. "He hit a winning streak at the tables." She sighed. "We got back a little while ago. I just found your note."

"Okay." What else could she say?

"Where are you, Jennifer?" Celia's voice was now tight with concern.

"I'm working for Marshall Grainger," Jen said, warmth spreading over her as she said Marsh's name out loud. She tried to snap herself out of it. "As I also wrote on my note."

"Jennifer Dunning," her mother said, sounding panicked, "I want to know exactly where you are living."

Lifting the phone from her ear, Jen stared at it in astonishment. The sound of her mother's obvious nervousness was shocking. Very little rattled her mother. She hesitated to reveal that she was living in Marsh's home, afraid her mother would really freak out.

"I'm living in Mr. Grainger's house," she said as calmly as she could, steeling herself for the explosion.

There was a quiet pause, then Celia went off like a rocket. "In his *house?* What house—here in Dallas? Are you out of your mind? Good heavens, Jennifer, have you any idea of that man's reputation?"

"I may not be socially inclined, Mother, but I'm not unconscious. Of course I'm aware of his reputation." Jen answered with hard-fought calm. "But I am here in the capacity of his assistant, not his mistress. And I'm staying in the housekeeper's quarters, in the back of the house," she tacked on reassuringly.

"But you already have a position here in Dallas."

Ignoring the sting of injured tears in her eyes, Jen said, "Mother, I quit my job over two weeks ago." She didn't add, *And you never noticed.*

"You did?"

Jen closed her eyes. "Yes, I did."

"But why didn't you tell me?" Celia demanded, her tone impatient.

"You were…busy, and I didn't want to interrupt." She cringed at the memory of discovering her parents' secret.

"But still, Jennifer, you could have told me."

Tears trickled down Jen's face but she was damned if she would allow her distress to show in her voice. "Well, I'm here now and enjoying the work."

"But where is here exactly?"

"Mr. Grainger's home is near Fredericksburg." There was no way Jen would reveal the location of the house, certain that if she did her mother would show up within a day or two.

"Jennifer." Impatience was strong in Celia's voice. "Where precisely—"

"Oh, I'm sorry," Jen interrupted her. "Mr. Grainger is calling. I have to go. We're very busy."

"But—"

Again Jen interrupted. "Mother, please, I must hang up now. You can call me again, or email me. Goodbye." She gently pressed the off button.

Jen wiped the tears from her eyes, realizing in that moment just how deeply it affected her that it had taken her parents so long to realize she was gone. She had indeed shocked them with her actions, but at this point, her mother's reaction felt like too little too late.

At some point, she would have to talk to them about

what had happened. But she wasn't going to be ready for that conversation anytime soon.

The rest of the week played out much the same as the first day in her office, except for one difference—and it was a big one.

On Tuesday, after serving dinner, Jen was about to take her meal up to her apartment when Marsh again asked her to join him. But this time, he actually started talking to her moments after she seated herself opposite him.

Of course, it was mainly talk about the ranch business, but that beat silence hands-down. She did have one problem, though—the quiet sound of his voice caused a quivery sensation inside her, and as if that wasn't enough, there seemed to be a constant hum of energy flowing between them, not only at the table but whenever they were in the same room. But based on his attitude, it obviously didn't mean a thing to him.

All in all, she'd become uneasy whenever he was around.

On the weekend, Jen barely saw anything of Marsh as she was busy cleaning and doing her laundry. A few times, when she was overheated, she had a swim before making a meal. She fell into a pattern of curling up with a book in the evening and ignoring her mother's phone calls. Jen had nothing to say for now.

The time seemed to fly by. After several more weeks of work during which Jen saw very little of Marsh, it came as a surprise one Saturday morning when, after clearing away the breakfast things, he stopped her as she headed for the laundry room.

"Jen," he said. "Do you ride?"

Blinking, Jen turned, laundry basket held in front of her. "What?"

"I asked if you ride," he said. "Horses."

"Oh, yes. Why?" She noticed a small smile twitching at the corners of his mouth.

"I'm going for a ride, to give the horses a run while getting some fresh air. I was wondering if you'd care to join me," he said. "Other than a few laps in the pool, we've both been inside all week."

Stunned by the sudden invitation, Jen could barely speak. She simply stared at him, trying not to be affected by the snug fit of his jeans clinging to his flat belly and his tight butt, the width of his shoulders beneath a chambray shirt, the sprinkling of hair on his forearms below the turned-back sleeves. She cautioned herself against accepting his invitation.

And then she accepted.

"I'd love to go," she said, ignoring for the moment how simply being near him affected her.

"Good." Marsh gave a quick nod and started for the kitchen door. "Leave the laundry until later."

"I need to change," Jen said, glancing down at the faded, torn clam-diggers she had put on to clean. "It'll only take a minute."

"I'll go saddle the horses." He stepped outside, hesitating before closing the door to say, "Take your time, I'm in no hurry."

As Jen headed to her apartment, her heart beating quickly from more than just the exercise of climbing the stairs, she wondered exactly what she'd just gotten herself into with Marsh Grainger.

Now, why in hell did I do that? Marsh thought, striding to the stables. Wasn't it hard enough merely sitting across the table from Jen, watching the smooth suppleness of her body as she moved around the kitchen?

He started saddling the mare he had chosen for her. When had he become a masochist? Marsh shook his head. He hadn't been with a woman in several months. Hell, he hadn't been off the property in weeks, not since he'd been to Houston. And he had come home from there frustrated and dissatisfied.

Finished saddling the mare, he turned to his mount. *What is it about Jen that is different from any other woman? And how many times have I asked myself that question since she moved in?* Marsh mused, throwing the saddle blanket over the back of his horse. Okay, she was beautiful—traffic-stopping beautiful—but he had met many beautiful women, a lot of them deeply in love...with themselves.

On the other hand, Jen didn't appear at all narcissistic or even impressed by her beauty. That was okay, he was impressed enough for both of them. She had a mouth made for kissing. The thought made him warm. Warm, hell, it made him hot. Mentally tamping down his sudden need, he directed his thoughts away from her lips to a more comfortable direction.

On reflection, Jen appeared down-to-earth and easygoing with a good sense of humor and an excellent work ethic, and her cooking could put most professional chefs' offerings to shame.

But the thing that really got to him was she sang while she worked. Even though her tone was soft it had filtered under his office door a few times. The sound had the power to cause a strange sensation inside him, bringing back old memories he hadn't thought about in years.

He was just a kid, a kid whose mother had left him

wondering what he had done to make her go. His father was so desolate he barely spoke to his son.

Fortunately, Marsh had had a friend from school. His name was Ben, a good kid whose mother, Marie, invited Marsh to come to their home whenever he wanted to go. And, with the constant gloom and doom in the house, Marsh was always ready to go.

Marie had a beautiful laugh, and she laughed a lot. It was a feel-good sound that touched something in him… just like Jen's singing.

Marsh had a startling realization. Practically everything Jen did evoked those warm sensations he had enjoyed in Ben's home. He knew Jen would make a good wife and an excellent mother—without straining he could almost hear her crooning to a baby.

This was what he was thinking when he looked down and realized Jen was standing next to him. All he could do was hope she wasn't a mind reader.

Jen had obviously caught Marsh deep in thought—she could tell from the faraway look on his face that he hadn't known she was there. She'd been pretty lost in thought herself the whole time she'd been changing into jeans, a pullover cotton sweater and low-heeled ankle boots. She'd grabbed a straw cowboy hat from a hook on the wall in the laundry room, and strode out into the beautiful October day, aware that her breath was coming a trifle quickly the closer she got to the stables—or rather, to Marsh.

He hadn't heard her come in, and for a moment, she'd just watched him standing by the horses, reins in one hand as he stroked the neck of the nearest animal with the other, an expression of deep contemplation on his face shadowed by the brim of his hat.

For an instant, Jen had wondered how it would feel to have his hand stroking her. She'd had that image in her head as she came to stand next to him. And when he turned to look at her, the expression on his face sent a sizzle up her spine, leaving her breathless.

"Ready to go?" he asked, handing a set of reins to her.

"Yes," she said, forcing her gaze from him to the horses. "They are beautiful animals," she murmured, moving forward to stroke the white star on the long head of her horse. She laughed as the shiny roan nuzzled her hand. "Morgan horses?"

"Yes," he answered, offering her a smile that set off the sizzle again. "Do you need help mounting?"

Jen shook her head, certain that if he touched her, however lightly, the sizzle would consume her. "Is she gentle?" Her voice was barely there. She cleared her throat.

Marsh frowned. "Yes. Is something wrong?"

"No…no." Feeling like a fool, she again shook her head. "I'm fine."

"Her name is Star." He shrugged. "Applicable, if not very original."

"I think it's perfect." Smiling, Jen moved to the left side of the horse, slipped her boot into the stirrup and swung her leg over into the saddle. She didn't realize until she settled into the leather that Marsh had mounted at exactly the same time.

He glanced over at her. His steely eyes held a silvery gleam. "Ready?"

"Yes." Jen nodded, suspicious of the meaning behind that gleam.

They moved off at a walk, which became a jog.

Marsh turned to look at her. "Are you up for a good run?"

"I'd love it," she said.

He took off.

Laughing, she was beside him within seconds. He flashed a grin, she returned it. The flat-out gallop was invigorating and ended much too soon. Marsh pulled his mount up beside a narrow stream and dismounted.

Jen did likewise, following as he led his horse to the water. "What's your horse's name?" she asked, looking over the sleek, dark brown gelding.

"Cocoa," he said, his tone serious.

"You're kidding." She couldn't help the laugh that escaped. "Cocoa?"

"Isn't that what his color looks like?" he said, "Dark, rich cocoa?"

"Yes, delicious dark chocolate, like your hair."

The words were out before she could catch herself. She had been looking at the horse, but her eyes instinctively found his. "I…uh…"

"Yours is golden-honey and looks like silk." His voice was low, almost a growl.

Jen was suddenly hot, an ache settling in the pit of her stomach. She stared at him in silence a moment, searching for something to say. "Th…thank…" Her throat went dry as he stepped close to her.

"You're beautiful." A wry smile played at the corners of his mouth. "But then you know that." He moved to within a breath of her. "Don't you?"

If only she could breathe. She managed to inhale. "Thank you." Surprise, she had managed that, too. "And you're right. I do know." She swallowed, quickly licking her lips. It didn't help—they dried again as his gaze followed the movement of her tongue. "I've been hearing it from the day I was born." He was standing too close, much too close. "But no one has said it quite like you."

"I want to kiss you."

"Wh...what?" Her chest felt tight. Her heart was thumping. The ache in her stomach swirled down to the core of her body. "Why?" *Dumb, Jen,* she thought.

"I want to taste you." His breath misted her lips. "I want to find out if you taste like honey."

Yes, yes, a murmur inside her head whispered as she trembled...and parted her lips.

Marsh didn't hesitate. Lowering his head, he touched his mouth to hers with gentle care. Then he slightly, tentatively deepened the kiss as he pulled her into a tight embrace. She made a soft sound in her throat. His mouth went hard to devour hers.

Oh, he is delicious, Jen mused fuzzily, curling her arms around his taut neck and spearing her fingers through the thick strands of his silky hair.

Releasing his hold on her, he stepped back, causing her arms to drop, her fingers to slide from his hair. He stared hard at her. "You taste good."

"You need a haircut." It was true, but Jen could have kicked herself for saying it. Still, that was better, she felt sure, than admitting his taste outdid anything she ever could have imagined.

"You're right." He laughed and raked his fingers through the wavy dark strands.

Jen loved the sound of his laughter, delighted she had been the cause of it, wanting to make him do it again, especially knowing how seldom he laughed.

They stood staring at each other for several long seconds. She wanted to fling herself back into his arms, take another taste of him, this time with her tongue.

She took a hesitant step toward him. Star chose that

moment to nudge her. She laughed and turned to pet the animal just as Cocoa gave a whinny.

"At the risk of sounding corny and cliché," she said, "I think the horses are getting restless. I guess we'd better head back."

Marsh nodded as he moved to Cocoa. "I have a few phone calls to make."

Jen mounted, and glanced back at Marsh. *Heavens*, she thought, *he looks magnificent on a horse*.

"Who do you think enjoys it more?" He raised an eyebrow. "You or the horse?"

Jen laughed, then, clicking her tongue to get Star moving, she called back to him, "Me."

As they galloped back to the stable, Jen could barely think of anything besides that kiss. But once they dismounted, everything went back to the status quo. Marsh handed the horses over to a man who suddenly appeared at his side, then without another word strode off to his office. Jen smiled at the man, assuming he was one of the security guards. Confused by the tumble of emotions inside her, Jen headed inside, started the laundry and went to her apartment to change before cleaning.

She undressed and put on the raggedy clam-diggers and shirt she'd had on earlier. She still planned on giving a quick brush-up to the first floor, but first, she needed a cup of coffee.

Marsh beat her to it.

When she walked into the kitchen the aroma of brewing coffee wafted to her. Marsh was standing at the stove, stirring something in a pot. Jen knew without looking that the pot held soup.

"I hope you don't mind me taking over your kitchen," he said, "and that you like vegetable soup." He slid a quick glance at her, his eyebrows arched.

"I don't mind you taking care of lunch at all," Jen replied, trying to sound as normal as possible though being close to him was making her body vibrate with the need to kiss him again. "I think I'll have a grilled cheese sandwich with my soup. Would you like one, too?"

"Sure." He gave a shadow of a smile. "Thanks." Marsh seemed as cool as could be. Obviously that kiss hadn't had half the effect on him that it had had on her.

Concentrating on the job at hand, she removed the bread from the cabinet. The faint sizzle that was still running laps up and down her spine slowly began to ease as she got to work—until she couldn't help but look over at Marsh, and found him looking right back at her with that impenetrable silver gaze.

Jen felt it all the way down to her toes.

She was in deep, deep trouble.

Four

"How many horses do you have?" *Oh, how brilliant,* she thought.

"Six," he answered.

"Do…er…you take care of them yourself?" *Again, brilliant,* she chastised herself.

Was the slight smile he gave her holding a tinge of ridicule or was it pity?

"No," he said. "Ted, a retired wrangler, cares for them. If you want to ride, see him. Whenever you're free."

"Oh, I see, thank you."

"Any other questions of the equine variety?" he asked, that smile twitching his lips.

Of course the twitch drew her attention to his mouth, which made her suddenly warm with memories of his kiss.

She wet her lips.

His gaze zeroed in on her mouth.

She grew warmer.

"No." Her voice was subdued.

They ate the rest of their meal in absolute silence.

"Coffee?" Marsh finally said.

"I'll get it." Jumping up, Jen went to fill two mugs with the steaming aromatic brew. He chuckled at her, that attractive masculine sound making her ache all over even as it annoyed her—he clearly felt he had the upper hand. She decided to throw him a curveball, just to see how he'd react.

"My mother called me last evening."

"That's nice."

"Well, actually it wasn't very pleasant," she admitted.

"Problems on the home front?"

"Yes," she said, eyeing him carefully. "My parents are having a problem with my living alone in this house with you."

He laughed outright.

Jen's insides went all soft at the sound. "You find that amusing?" Well, it was pretty funny. Her mother and father, of all people. Of course, he was unaware of that nasty situation.

"My reputation precedes me," he said, his laughter fading. "I hope you assured her you're safe here."

Without pausing to think, Jen said, "Am I?"

"I assume you're referring to that kiss earlier." His tone was dry.

"Yes," she answered, meeting his steady gaze with a challenging stare.

"There was a reason for it," he said, suddenly all business.

"What reason?" Jen couldn't imagine what he was referring to.

"It was a test." His silvery gaze held her in confused thrall.

She frowned. "I don't understand."

"I want a child, an heir—better yet two."

He spoke so calmly, Jen was stumped for a moment. When his meaning sunk in, she actually yelped. *"What?"*

"Oh, don't be alarmed, you passed."

"What do you mean, I passed?"

"The kiss test," he said. "You passed with flying colors."

"I still don't get it. What is a 'kiss test,' and what does it have to do with heirs?"

"I've decided you'd make not only a good lover but a good wife and mother," he explained casually. "Of course there's more to good sex than a great kiss."

Jen was flabbergasted. Her throat had gone so dry she had to pause to swallow. "Are you proposing to me…or propositioning me?"

He gave her a wicked smile, his silver eyes shimmering. "Both."

Jen glanced around the room as if seeking help. Finding none, she picked up her mug, unsure whether she wanted to drink from it or throw it at him. "This is insane."

"What's insane about wanting a child?" He stood, and came to lean against her side of the table. He was close—too close.

Jen had to raise her head to look at him. "Nothing," she said. "It's your way of going about it that's strange. Now back up."

"What?" He frowned.

"I said back up." Jen's tone was more order than request. "I want to stand up." He obliged, and she stood and turned but he caught her arm, bringing her to a halt.

"I'd much rather we go upstairs and test our physical compatibility."

Jen stared at him a moment as she would a being from another planet, torn between wanting to shut him down—and wanting to go upstairs with him so she could have his mouth on hers again. Finally she asked, "Are you nuts?"

Rather than the anger she expected, Marsh treated her to his insides-melting laugh.

"I like you," he said. "You're as prickly as I am. I believe we could make a go of it."

"Of what? A marriage of convenience?" Jen somehow managed to keep her voice calm.

"Yes." He nodded.

"Whose?"

"What do you mean, whose?" He appeared perplexed.

"My convenience…or yours?" She lost the battle for control of her voice. "Are you looking for a 'me Tarzan, you Jane' kind of arrangement?" She gave a quick, firm shake of her head. "No, thank you."

She pulled her arm from his to walk away. He grabbed her again.

"Damn you, let me go." She yanked her arm only to almost fall as he released her at the same instant. Reacting at once, he caught and steadied her.

"I'm sorry, was I hurting you?" His expression held genuine concern.

Jen drew a deep breath before answering. "No, but you're ticking me off big-time." She took another quick breath. "Now, like it or not, I am going to do some work." She glared at him. "Got that?"

She could tell he held back another laugh. "Yes, I think I've got that."

"Good." She studied him for a second. Damn, why did those lips, that mouth, those hands make her so crazy? And why did those very attributes tempt her to agree to his outrageous suggestion? "Please," she said, cringing at the near plea in her voice, "go somewhere, anywhere but here. I don't need an audience to clean."

With that, she strode to the laundry room, dumped the first load of wash from the washer into the dryer and got her cleaning supplies from the storage closet. A combined sigh of relief and regret whispered through her lips as she walked back into the kitchen to find he wasn't there.

She came to a dead stop when she found him waiting for her in the living room.

Eyeing him warily, she arched one brow.

"First, I am not looking for a 'me Tarzan, you Jane' relationship." He took a step closer to her and stared down at her. She felt her face flush against her will. "What I'm looking for—"

Jen knew she couldn't let him finish that sentence.

Dropping the cleaning products where she stood, she headed for the stairs.

"Where are you going?" he asked, sounding genuinely confused.

"Out," she called back, taking the stairs two at a time to get away from Marsh Grainger and his too-tempting proposition as fast as she could.

Five

"The hell with it," Marsh muttered as he strode through the house, seeking refuge in his office.

Dammit, the woman was driving him crazy. Was she coming back for dinner? Was she coming back at all? For an instant Marsh felt his stomach tighten at the idea of her leaving for good.

She was great at her job—all her jobs. He couldn't afford to lose her.

What had he done?

He sighed. He had spooked her by jumping the gun with his "test kiss" business. Well, in all honesty, he had startled himself, as well. He had never been the impulsive type. But ever since she'd walked into his life, he'd been doing nothing but acting on impulse. The idea of the two of them getting together on a permanent basis had been brewing at the back of his mind for days—and getting stronger with every touch, every conversation.

Why not? he had asked himself. She obviously wasn't involved with any other man, seeing as how she never mentioned anyone and hadn't left the house except to go shopping since she had started working for him.

Still, he probably should have given the idea more thought, given her more time to get to know him, which was his reason for inviting her to ride with him that morning in the first place.

And why was he beating himself up like this? It was so…so not like him.

Facing the bare truth, Marsh admitted he was burning to be with her, to make love to her. He had been observing her from the very beginning. Along with a growing respect for her, along with the feelings he experienced listening to her sing softly while she was working… He had entered the house from the stable one very warm Saturday afternoon and stopped in his tracks as he passed through the dining room. Hot and sweaty, he had stood there, transfixed by the sight of Jen getting out of the pool, water sluicing the length of her slender body barely covered by a string bikini.

In that instant he was not only hot and sweaty, he was rock hard and hurting. He wanted her so badly his back teeth ached…along with the rest of him.

It was during the days following that encounter that Marsh began thinking about bargaining with Jen, offering her his name, his home, his bed in exchange for a child. Finally, he had decided to take a chance—and for him to take a chance with a woman, even a woman such as Jen, was a huge step for him.

Had he botched his chances with his abrupt actions and suggestions? A "test kiss"? Another "test" to see if they would be good together in bed? He grimaced.

Not the most romantic approach. But he had never had any trouble romancing a woman before.

Of course, Jen wasn't just any woman. She was different, special.

Dammit.

He couldn't blame her if she had left for good.

Had she taken all her things? She had had ample time as she hadn't brought very many with her. Hell, she wouldn't need to take anything but herself—she could send for her belongings, or have someone else come for them.

He'd really made a mess of things.

Sighing, he picked up the phone and made a few work calls. Then he sat in front of his computer, watching the cursor blink, as if impatient for him to decide what he was going to do. He put it to sleep.

Just then, the phone on his desk rang. He slid a glance at the caller ID, and eased back into his chair.

"Yes, Jen?" Marsh was pleased at the casual note he had managed.

"Can you handle dinner on your own?"

"Why?" he asked, heaving a put-upon sigh.

"I'm going to run into San Antonio and have dinner there, along the River Walk," she explained.

"Why don't I join you for dinner?" Marsh said. "I think maybe I need to explain a few things to you." He actually held his breath while waiting for her answer—that had *never* before happened to him with any woman.

"Well…"

Before she had a chance to say no he rushed on. "We could have dinner and then stroll along the River Walk or take a boat ride." The moments crawled by. He was holding his breath again.

"Okay," she said. "What time should I meet you?"

"Would six-thirty or seven work?"

"Seven would be fine. I'll see you then." Her voice came over the line hurried, a bit rough. "Bye."

Marsh's breathing slowly returned to normal. Could their having dinner together away from the house be considered a date? Marsh thought about it for a moment. He supposed it definitely could—if he hadn't just scared her out of the house with his proposition.

Hell, he mused, what was he getting all worked up about? He knew how to go about charming a woman— he had charmed his share, maybe more than his share. So why sweat it? He could begin over dinner, and probably have Jen eating from his hand by…

No. He couldn't, wouldn't, approach Jen as if she were any other woman. She wasn't.

So no seduction, unless it happened completely naturally, he told himself. This date was simply a way for him to back up and make amends to the employee he was so desperate to hold on to.

Of course it was.

Jen slipped the cell phone into the side pocket of her shoulder bag as she walked out into the golden sunlight from the cool, soothing interior of the Mission Alamo.

No matter how many times she visited San Antonio, the first thing she did was head for the old mission. Although traffic was busy on the broad street so close to the complex, inside it was always quiet, and on the hottest days, it seemed cool. There was a sense of peace and calm inside the Alamo Jen had never experienced anywhere else. And she had always thought how lovely it would be to be married inside that quiet and serene old shrine.

It could happen if she agreed to Marsh's proposal.

Jen shook her head. The thought of wearing his ring, sharing his bed, bearing his child—it was so very tempting. But she couldn't stand the idea of living with him knowing he didn't love her, and not knowing if she could love him.

It was absurd to even be thinking about Marsh in that way.

Wasn't it?

Waiting for the light to change so she could cross the street, she glanced down, frowning slightly at the tremor in her hands. Speaking to Marsh, agreeing to meet him for dinner had shaken that inner peace, ruffled her sense of calm.

Why had she called him in the first place?

Wait a minute, she thought, trying to get control of her thoughts. *Why in the world should I feel nervous about having agreed to meet Marsh for dinner? We not only have dinner but every meal together in the house— his house—three times a day, every day.*

But this wasn't the house, she mused. And there was the small matter of the fact that he had proposed to her.

This was a date. A Saturday-night date. And on this particular Saturday he had kissed her, and asked her to go to his bed…and have his child!

All of it gave Jen pause. A date with Marsh? A marriage with him? A *life* with him? She'd barely let herself want him, or imagine a future beyond right now. Was a long-term relationship something she wanted?

Maybe.

She couldn't suppress the thrill of anticipation that skidded the length of her spine just thinking about the possibilities.

Oh, yes, he was what she wanted, she finally conceded, and *he wanted her*. The thought lodged in her mind as she crossed the bridge to the River Walk.

He had admitted as much, she thought, ambling along, unconscious of the throngs of people around her. Well, he didn't actually say he wanted *her*. He said he wanted a child—an heir, maybe two.

Not quite the words a woman wants to hear when receiving a marriage proposal. Hell, she mused, she had once received a fervent proposal from a young man who had actually dropped onto one knee to pledge his undying love for her.

Marsh's proposal was a far cry from that.

Jen strolled into the Rivercenter Mall and headed straight for Victoria's Secret without even realizing what she was doing. She was looking through the sales tables when she glanced up, her gaze caught by a mannequin. The nightgown was barely there and what *was* there was flame-red.

On the spot, Jen motioned to a nearby smiling sales clerk and bought the sinful-looking gown.

She wouldn't admit that she was thinking about Marsh as she did so.

Jen left the mall and made her way to the restaurant. She started when a hand touched hers, taking her bag from her.

"Hey—" she began, turning to glare at the person.

"You're late," Marsh drawled.

Jen somehow managed to keep from rolling her eyes. "I was shopping and lost sight of the time."

"Obviously," he said.

"Oh, lighten up," Jen retorted.

While imperiously arching a brow he gave way to a smile. He shot a cuff to look at his watch. "We're five minutes late."

"How very sophisticated of us," she murmured. "I hope they are duly impressed."

"Nah," Marsh said, shaking his head. "They probably expect us to be late."

Surprised and amused by his casual tone, Jen gave a soft laugh. "What if we aren't late enough and we have to wait for a table?"

Marsh slanted a positively wicked look at her. "It ain't gonna happen, kid. The name's Grainger, remember?" He opened the door for her. "Besides, I know the owner and chef."

The place was medium-size, the décor blending with the River Walk theme. The food was superb, the service outstanding.

Jen barely noticed.

It occurred to her that it was strikingly different being out with Marsh than sitting opposite him at his kitchen table. Here, tonight, Marsh captivated her. He was…everything she had ever thought a man should be.

Handsome, urbane, but most importantly, intelligent. His intelligence shone from his silvery eyes, along with a keen sense of humor she had never heard mentioned about him before. Had most people missed it? Jen didn't see how it was possible for anyone to miss what was right there in front of them. At times, his eyes fairly danced with the light of devilish humor.

Why did he have to turn out to be a womanizer? Or was he? If the gossipmongers had missed Marsh's sense of humor, had they misread other things about him, as well?

Beware of wishful thinking, she told herself.

"What are you thinking?" he asked.

Marsh was sitting with his forearms on the table, cradling his after-dinner brandy. His hands moved slowly, warming the potent liquid. She wondered if this was the moment when he was going to explain himself to her.

"About you," she admitted.

One dark eyebrow arched. "What about me?"

He lowered his head. His lips parted to sip the brandy. Jen felt she could actually taste his lips, the tang of the brandy on them.

"Oh," she said with a delicate shrug, "I'm just wondering exactly what it is you wanted to talk about tonight."

He chuckled and the sound seemed to go right through her.

He took another sip, keeping his eyes on her. "I feel I might have offended you with my…business proposal."

Jen nearly spit out her wine. "Is that what that was?"

He nodded. "It was. I'm a businessman, Jen. When I see something that looks like a good, smart opportunity, I take it."

Her heart skittered a little at the idea of being "taken" by Marsh. By the glint in his eye, she could tell that was exactly what he wanted her to be thinking.

"But like I said, I'm sorry if I offended you."

Jen couldn't help but wonder, as she sat there looking at the gorgeous Marsh Grainger, how many other women he had presented with his "business" proposal. But then, how many women could a man possibly meet if he spent all his time at home, in his house?

"Why do you hide out in your home instead of working in your office in Dallas?"

For a moment—a long moment—she was certain he had no intention of answering her. In fact, she was steeling herself for a rebuke.

"I get more done that way."

Jen was a little startled at his blunt admittance. A

tiny frown tugging her brows together, she asked, "You can get more work done alone than you can surrounded by people to assist you?"

He nodded, tipping the glass to finish off his drink. "I do have people—too many people—around me to assist. I prefer the quiet of my office at the house. On the other hand—"

He was interrupted by their server asking if he could get something else for them.

"No, thank you, just the check," Marsh said, his gaze steady on Jen's face. "Are you going to finish your wine?"

"No." Jen shook her head, a small smile playing on her lips. "I'm driving."

Turning from her, he took care of the check. Then he circled the table to hold her chair for her.

"You were saying," Jen prompted him as soon as they were back outside. As they walked, the crowds had to go around them—it didn't hurt that Marsh was such an imposing, intimidating man.

"On the other hand," he said, strolling beside her, unaware of the impatient looks of some of the people having to skirt around them. "There are times I have to go into Dallas or Houston for important meetings."

"As you did the weekend I started working for you," she recalled aloud.

He hesitated, a half smile shadowing his lips for an instant. "Yes," he said, his tone wry.

Now, what was that all about? The man was certainly an enigma. If she thought about everything that had happened between them in one day, it practically made her head spin. First a kiss, then…a proposal.

A proposal was serious business. Was she seriously considering it?

"Hello, Jennifer." Marsh's softened voice drew her from introspection. "We're here."

Here? Where? Blinking herself back from the realm of Marsh's hot kiss and the proposal to the present, Jen was startled to find herself standing next to her car. Now, how in the world had he known where she had parked?

"How did you…"

"I looked."

"You looked?" She stared at him in amazement. "All the places to park around here, and you not only looked for my car, you spotted it?"

Marsh shrugged. "It's pretty hard to miss an old, dusty white Caddy, even at dusk."

Although Jen took offense at his description of the vehicle she loved, she let it slide for the moment. "Okay, so where did you park?"

"Back there a few blocks. You wait here while I go get it and I'll follow you home."

"I know the way home, Marsh," she said.

"I know you do," he replied. "But I'm still following you back to the ranch, so you wait here. That's an order, Jennifer. I can't have you disappearing on me— we're not quite done talking yet. And we need some privacy to do it."

And with that, he just turned and walked away.

Six

Jen was fuming. Certain smoke was rising from her ears, she stared after Marsh. Who the hell did he think he was?

Well, yeah, he was her boss—he was boss to a lot of people, she reluctantly conceded—but that didn't give him the right to issue orders to her on a date. Sighing, she nevertheless slid behind the wheel of the Caddy like a good and obedient employee.

Anger seared through her.

Her day had been a whirlwind, starting with their ride. There was the kiss, and the perplexing and—if she was being totally honest with herself—rather flattering proposal. She had enjoyed their ride to the stream. She had enjoyed the horses. She had even enjoyed Marsh's kiss.

Who was she kidding? She hadn't just enjoyed his

kiss, she had melted into it, and wanted more when it was over…only to hear him tell her it had been a test.

A test! As if that were not bad enough, he proceeded to ask her to have sex with him to make certain they would be good together in bed. And if it so happened they *were* compatible as lovers, he then would marry her, simply because he considered her good wife and mother material, mother being the most important role as he needed an heir to inherit his vast wealth and would prefer two children. Like royalty, she supposed—an heir and a spare.

She'd been thinking about that proposal all day. But damned if now, after their first date, she wasn't quite sure how she felt.

Especially since he'd just ordered her around.

Jen didn't realize she was gritting her teeth until she heard the sound of a horn and glanced at the side mirror to see Marsh pulled up alongside the car parked behind her. Starting the engine, she eased out onto the street and drove ahead of him.

He stayed on her tail, as if their bumpers were locked, all the way back to the ranch. Jen had the whole drive to work up a full head of angry steam at the way he had again managed to confuse, excite and befuddle her all in one day.

She tried to untangle the emotions in her head. How did she feel about Marsh? She had enjoyed having dinner with him—he had been good company. The conversation they had engaged in had been amusing.

So, what was she *really* fuming about?

Jen knew full well what she was really fuming about—her growing attraction to a man who wanted to give her a compatibility test. But it was so much easier to tell herself she was annoyed by his arrogant demand that she wait for him to follow her back to the ranch.

It was as good an excuse as anything else she could come up with on the spur of the moment.

As Jen drove past the two stone pillars on either side of the road to the house, she thrust her arm out the window in a wave and gave a quick honk of the horn in greeting to the guard, as she had been doing every time she left or returned to the ranch. The guard gave a honk and flashed his lights in response.

Watching for it, she noticed neither Marsh nor the guard acknowledged one another.

She was not surprised; she imagined he saw no reason to greet his employees every time he left or returned to the property. He paid his people very well—Jen knew because she cut the checks, her own included. She presumed he figured that was acknowledgement enough. And it had been, for her. Until he'd broken their delicate truce with that kiss.

And that proposal.

Suddenly tired, Jen pulled into the space Marsh had allotted her in the garage and killed the engine. Marsh pulled into the slot next to her. A deflated sigh whispered through her lips as she got out of the car and walked to the trunk to retrieve her shopping bag.

"Let me help you with that," he said, plucking the Victoria's Secret bag from her fingers. *If he only knew what's in that bag,* she thought.

He trailed her through the doors and up the stairs to her apartment. As she never locked the door, she walked right inside and turned to relieve him of the bag.

Marsh was right behind her and closed the door with a quiet but definite click.

Jen arched her brows in question.

"Aren't you going to offer me a reward for carrying your bag?" he asked.

"Reward?" Her brows lowered while her eyes narrowed. "What sort of reward?"

He almost smiled.

He'd been smiling all day. She wondered if it had hurt his lips, then chided herself for the snide thought.

"Coffee, wine, something stronger?"

"Something stronger, huh?" Jen asked in a wry tone. "You wouldn't be thinking of getting me tipsy, would you?"

Marsh made it all the way to a real smile this time. "Not at all, coffee will be fine. The last thing I want is for your mind to be cloudy when I take you to bed."

His response stopped her cold. Well, not exactly— while it gave her chills on the surface of her skin, it ignited a blaze inside her.

She was silent for a moment, staring into the heat burning in the depths of his eyes. Coming to her senses, she said, "Excuse me?"

"I think you heard me."

"I thought we had more 'talking' to do, Mr. Grainger."

"We do. But it's a very special kind of talking," he said, giving her a smile so charming she felt it all the way down to her toes.

She broke eye contact and hurried away, into the kitchen.

"Coffee will take only a few minutes. Make yourself comfortable." Jen was amazed at how calm and composed she sounded, when what she was feeling was confused and, yes, so turned on she could hardly breathe.

She spilled coffee grounds from the measuring spoon as her trembling fingers dumped them into the basket.

She also spilled a few drops of water as she poured the water into the well.

Damn, she thought, what was it about Marsh that could rattle her so easily? Okay, he was handsome in a rough-hewn, chiseled way. But he was too arrogant and full of himself. His reputation with women was less than sterling, a living, breathing bad boy.

Except in his case he was most definitely a man.

She had read somewhere that every woman wanted to be the one to tame a bad boy. At the time, Jen had expelled a very unladylike snort of derision.

Yeah, she had thought at the time, that was what she lived for—being one of whatever number of eager females in line to tame a bad boy.

Why would any woman think that—after who knew how many a womanizer had been with before—*she* would be the one to bring him to heel and keep him there? More to the point, Jen mused, why would she want to?

If he's as hot as Marsh... said a little voice in her head.

Had Marsh Grainger managed to change her stance on bad boys?

"Coffee ready?"

Jen jumped but managed to swallow the yelp of surprise that sprang to her lips.

Marsh was standing behind her, close, too close. She gathered her composure as she drew a quick breath.

"Yes." Jen was satisfied with the even tone she had managed. "It only takes a few minutes for—" She stiffened, her voice cutting off completely. He had lifted her long hair away from her shoulder.

"What are you doing?"

Brilliant. She knew exactly what he was doing.

"Smelling you," he murmured, slowly inhaling her scent. "You smell good."

The tip of his tongue touched the sensitive skin near the back of her ear. She grew cold, and then hot. "M… Marsh?"

"You taste good, too." His tongue slid the length of her neck to the curve of her shoulder.

Jen gasped as suddenly he turned her around to face him. "Marsh…you… I…"

"I want you, Jennifer. I've wanted you since I set eyes on you and that kiss only made me want you more." Lowering his head he brushed her mouth with his, gliding his tongue along her bottom lip. "And I think you want me, too."

"I…I don't… Oh!" She trembled as he moved, pressing his body to hers. "You shouldn't…"

He did. Cradling her face with his hands, he again touched his mouth to hers. His kiss was gentle, sweet, soft.

Knowing she should resist, push him back, away from her overheating body, Jen instead surrendered to the neediness gnawing inside her. Curling her arms around his taut shoulders, she gave up her mouth to him.

Marsh took her mouth, owned it, claimed it with the thrust of his tongue, and in that instant she was his. Bad boy or not.

So much for her brave words about resisting a womanizer. Too late…she was lost.

Later, Jen would wonder how they had managed to leave a trail of clothing from the kitchen to her bedroom without once breaking that kiss.

When at last he lifted his mouth from hers, they were both naked, heaving in deep breaths of air. Shivering, tiny hitches of breath still catching in her throat, Jen stared into his eyes, fascinated by the blaze of desire she found in their depths.

Without a word, Marsh tossed back the top sheet and puffy white comforter she had bought for her bed. Then he reached for her, gently settling her on the smooth white sheet in the center of the mattress, stretching his long, hard body next to her.

"I was going to ask you to put on that pretty little red nightgown you bought for tonight, but I think I like you better like this," he growled.

Jen felt herself turning bright red at the image of Marsh looking in that bag while she'd been in the kitchen making coffee. She wanted to insist that she hadn't bought the nightgown for tonight, but she wasn't sure if that was true or not. And it certainly didn't matter now.

Marsh caressed her jawline, outlined her lips with his fingers. His touch was so very gentle yet so very arousing. Jen lifted her head, inviting his kiss.

"Yes," he murmured, lowering his head to glide his tongue over her lips, then fusing his mouth to hers.

Jen loved the taste of him. His long, deepening kiss made her ache for more. She slid her free arm around his neck and thrust her fingers into his hair.

A low sound of pleasure whispered from her mouth into his when his left hand slowly moved from the curve of her neck to the curve of her breast. Leaving her mouth, his lips followed the path of his hand.

Jen was on fire inside. She moaned and arched her back when his tongue gently lashed the now hard tip of her breast. A moment later she arched her hips as his hand moved down her body to cup her mound before inserting one finger inside her. In the next instant, a soft cry spilled from her throat as he brushed his thumb over the most sensitive spot there.

In her mind, Jen saw herself as a flame, burning higher and higher just for him. She arched again, harder against his hand, into his teasing fingers.

Straightening his arm resting against the bed, Marsh moved his long body to cover hers, cradling himself between her thighs.

She could feel him, the length of him, the hardness of him nudging the entrance to her body. She moved in silent invitation for him to enter.

With one swift, deep thrust he was inside her, tightly, uncomfortably filling her.

Jen expelled an involuntary cry of pain as her body tensed and stiffened.

He froze in place, shock in his silvery eyes.

"What is it? Have I hurt you?" His voice was strained.

Before she could respond, he said in a tone of near disbelief, "Are you…a virgin?"

Jen's harsh breaths were beginning to ease. "No… no, I'm not a virgin." She drew a deep, calm breath. He began to withdraw. She grasped his hips with her hands, holding him in place. "No," she repeated, the tension now easing from her body.

"If I'm too big for you…" Concern colored his voice, not quite hiding a hint of disappointment.

"It's okay." She offered him a small smile. "I'm adjusting. It'll be all right." She curled her legs around his waist, holding him to her. "Just give me a moment."

"Okay," he agreed, his expression puzzled, his voice a little breathless. "You want to tell me what happened there?"

"It's been a while since I've been with a man, that's

all," she said, adding with a little laugh, "and you're big."

"And you're tight," he said, desire flaring in his eyes.

Jen maintained his gaze, watching it change as she started to move her hips slowly, seductively against him. The flame inside her was quickly flaring to life again as her body relaxed, adjusting to the new sensation of the fullness of him.

Fleetingly, she recalled her painful though limited experience while still in college. In comparison to Marsh… In truth, there was no comparison. Wanting more, Jen moved against him, letting him know she was ready.

Exhaling a long sigh, Marsh began to move with her, his expression still wary but his body eager for hers. He began slow and easy, but with the urgent feel of her fingernails digging into his hips, he increased his tempo.

Faster. Deeper. More, more, Jen demanded with her body, claiming him as he claimed her. Tension tightened inside her, driving her wild. "Faster. Deeper." She didn't even realize she had cried aloud.

Marsh was with her, every literal inch of the way. It was building inside his body. Jen could feel him keeping pace with her, getting closer and closer to the edge. Her strained breaths were keeping time with his.

Gazing up at him—at the tautness of his face, at the tendons standing out in his arched neck—excited her, gave her the will to wait for him.

The world exploded for both of them. They cried out as if with one voice. Never in her life had Jen experienced anything so all-consuming, so carnal and beautiful, so completely fulfilling.

Easing his body down to hers, Marsh buried his face in the curve of her neck. Jen circled her arms around his sweat-slicked shoulders. Ever since that fumbling, inept jock in college, she had been afraid she could never experience the sheer pleasure she had heard about, read about in books. Her fears were the main reason she had tried so hard to keep her distance from men— from Marsh.

Foolish woman.

"That was wonderful." Jen was so satiated and content she was barely aware of speaking the words aloud.

Marsh lifted his head to look at her, his eyes now a soft gray. "That was way more than wonderful," he said between slowly leveling breaths. "That, lady mine, was absolutely mind-blowing."

Lady mine. Jen shivered, wondering if he called all the women he had been with "lady mine."

"You're cold." Easing himself from her, he sat up and pulled the comforter over them. Curling his arm around her, he drew her body to him. "Better?"

"Yes." Jen sighed. It was true, it was better. In spite of all the rumors, the chattered gossip about him, she felt warm, safe and at home in his arms. She knew it was temporary—*she* was probably temporary, unless she accepted his crazy proposal. But she didn't want to think about that.

For now, she was content.

But her contentment lasted all of a few moments.

"Okay, let's hear it." His voice, though quiet, was demanding.

Jen lifted her head from his chest to frown at him. "Hear what?"

"You said it had been a while since you'd been with a man. Exactly how long is a while?"

Jen wet her lips, thinking *Dammit.* And she had been so comfortable. "I don't think that is really any of your business," she said, dredging up her most haughty tone of voice.

Marsh appeared less than impressed. "It is now. So tell me."

"And if I choose not to?"

His arm tightened around her. "I'll keep you right here in the bed until you do."

Jen blinked. "You wouldn't."

He smiled. "Try me."

Standoff. Jen knew he meant what he said. Still it bugged her to give in to him, even though she had obviously given in to him in a much bigger way mere minutes ago. Of course, that was different—her body had made that decision for her.

She heaved a dramatic sigh.

"Oh, brother," he drawled. "What's the big deal? Tell me and get it over with, then we can both get some sleep."

He hesitated, adding with a wicked grin, "Maybe."

Maybe? Jen felt a twinge of excitement zinging through her. Did he mean…? Of course that was what he meant, she chided herself.

"The big deal is," she began, trying and failing to ignore the flame that was very quickly coming back to life inside her, "I hadn't been with a man since my senior year in college."

Marsh jackknifed to sit up, staring down at her in shock. "That would be how many years ago?"

"It doesn't matter anymore," she said, impatiently. "Do you want to hear about it or sit there staring openmouthed at me in disbelief?"

"I didn't say I didn't believe you," he shot back at her. "Even though you must admit that is hardly the norm for a woman like you."

It was Jen's turn to sit up and glare at him eye to eye. "What do you mean, a 'woman like me'? What kind of woman would that be?" she demanded, completely unaware of her exposed breasts.

"A gorgeous, sexy, incredibly responsive woman." He was glaring right back at her. Even his glare was turning her on.

She lowered her eyes. "You think I'm gorgeous and sexy?" Jen knew full well she was beautiful, but hearing it from Marsh…well…the flame inside her burned even hotter.

"You know damn well you are both those," he retorted. "You're also exciting and good company and have a great sense of humor." His brows shot up. "Okay?"

"Yes," she murmured, glancing up at him. The comforter had dropped to their waists but the shiver that coursed through Jen's body had more to do with his compliments than the chill in the air. "You're not bad yourself," she said, daring to hold his bold stare.

Marsh actually laughed. "Thanks." Taking her with him, he lay down again, pulling her to him before tucking the comforter around them again.

"Okay, Jennifer," he said, tilting her face up to plant a kiss on her lips. "Talk to me."

"It's almost funny now, but at the time it was anything but," she began. "He was a jock…of course," she continued. "I had been curious about sex, as all my friends seemed to talk about it exclusively. Yet up until that point I hadn't felt attracted to any man." She wasn't about to elaborate—she had worked too hard to forget that incident in the school parking lot to dredge it up now, here, with Marsh.

Expecting some sort of wry remark from him, possibly concerning her sexual proclivities, she raised her gaze to his. His expression was attentive, free of either ridicule or disbelief.

Encouraged, she rushed on to relay the whole stupid incident to him and have it over with. "What had attracted me to him was that he was not only athletic, he was very nice as well as intelligent." She paused, wincing as the memory played in her mind.

"Go on." His voice was soft, kind. Jen was aware that she was seeing a side of Marsh she hadn't seen before, and it touched her.

"I agreed to go out with him," she said. "It wasn't a big deal, just to the Pizza and Beer Joint—which, by the way, is the actual name of the place. I had one glass of beer with my pizza, and he had five. He wasn't drunk," she added, "only a little tipsy and talkative."

She paused, the memory uncomfortably vivid. "At least I thought he wasn't drunk." She closed her eyes. "How's that saying go…he holds his booze well?"

Again Marsh tilted her head up to gaze into her eyes. "Jennifer, I have a distinct feeling you have never told another person about this encounter. Am I right?"

She answered with a quick nod of her head.

"Figured." His voice actually held a note of compassion. "You know," he continued softly, "I'm convinced you'll feel better if you get it out in the open once and for all. And I promise I won't alert the media immediately after you've finished," he teased.

She smiled, chiding herself for feeling stupid over an error in judgment years ago. Knowing Marsh was right she drew a deep breath and went on.

"Walking back to my off-campus room he put his arm around my waist and drew me against him. Although he was still talking away, his steps were steady, even. When we got to my room, he just walked in as if it were his own. I opened my mouth to protest, he silenced me with his lips pressing hard against mine."

Jen grabbed another breath before rushing on. "I really didn't mind the kiss—I rather liked it. But within seconds he had me flat on my back on the bed. His hands were everywhere, his tongue was scouring the inside of my mouth."

She paused for a moment.

"I tried to push him away, if only to breathe. When I began to struggle he lifted his head. His breathing was short and raspy, his voice raw as he said how badly he wanted me beneath him. Yanking my pullover up, he opened the front clasp of my bra and took my breast into his mouth. While shocked, I must admit the feel of his wet mouth on my breast sent an exciting sensation through me."

Jen halted once more to catch her breath.

"Jen, you don't have to—" Marsh began. She could hear anger in his tone, anger at the guy who had taken advantage of her.

"No—" she cut him off "—let me finish now or I might never finish."

He stayed quiet.

She continued. "He didn't rape me, if that's what you were thinking. I was willing, almost eager to experience the incredible pleasure every female I knew had raved about incessantly. He was eager, too—overeager. He yanked my jeans off and merely dropped his to his ankles. Then, well, it wasn't good." She closed her eyes. "Can we leave it at that?"

Marsh tightened his arm around her and held her, rocking her slightly side to side while smoothing her hair.

"It's over, Jennifer." His voice was soft, soothing, with underlying concern. "Did I hurt you like that?"

Jen pushed back against his hold so she could look up at him. "No." She shook her head. "After that initial discomfort and adjustment to you, I…I…"

"You what?" Marsh murmured, gliding his hand from her hair to her back.

Gathering herself, Jen boldly met his intent gaze. "I enjoyed it. I more than enjoyed it. It was…" She hesitated before admitting, "It was incredibly fantastic."

"Yeaaah," he said softly, drawing the word out. "Wanna do it again?"

Laughing softly, Jen freed her arms, clasped them around his neck and drew his mouth to hers. "Yes, please."

The second time was even better.

They fell asleep locked in each other's arms.

Seven

Jen woke a little after five in the morning. It was pitch-black in the room. Not wanting to wake Marsh, she refrained from lighting the bedside lamp, but to no avail. He woke while she was carefully disentangling herself from him.

"What are you doin'?" he mumbled, reaching for her.

Tossing back the covers she escaped his reach by slipping from the bed. "I'm going to the bathroom. I'll only be a moment. Go back to sleep."

Once inside the bathroom, Jen knew she would be in there longer than a moment—the shower looked so inviting, and she felt so pleasantly achy.

After cleaning off what was left of her makeup and brushing her teeth, she stepped into the shower, sighing with pleasure as the warm water cascaded over her body.

While she was drying off, Jen noticed a shirt of

Marsh's hanging on the back of the door. Now feeling a little awkward walking around nude, she pulled on the shirt before leaving the room. She stopped dead at the sight that met her eyes on her first step into her bedroom.

Stark naked, Marsh was leaning back against the headboard amidst the tangle of bedsheets and covers that had slid out of place during their rather hectic bout of sensual exercise.

"What are you doing?"

One browed arched. "Waiting for you." His voice was both wry and dry. "More to the point, why are you dressed?"

"I'm not fully dressed," she returned, every bit as wryly and dryly. "I'm only wearing a shirt."

"Not for long," he retorted, a sly smile crossing his face as his gaze traveled up and down her body.

"Indeed?" Jen said, trying and failing to ignore the tingle along her spine.

"Yes, indeed." He clasped his hands behind his head.

"Aren't you going to shower?" she asked the first thought that swam into her squishy brain.

"I think there's plenty of time for that later." He offered her a blatantly sexy smile. "Lose the shirt, lady mine, and come back to bed."

Jen was surprised to discover just how happy she was to toss off the shirt and crawl into the bed next to him.

As before, Marsh pulled her tightly against him. Then, to her surprise, he gave her a soft, sweet kiss, settled into his comfort place and whispered, "Sleep in tomorrow."

She felt a moment of disappointment, and then suddenly felt as if she couldn't keep her eyes open. Resting her head on his chest, she was asleep within seconds.

Jen woke later to discover she was alone in the bed and it was past ten in the morning. It was Sunday, a perfect day for sleeping in. For a moment, she considered snuggling deeper into the comforter but a rumble in her stomach made the decision for her. She was hungry.

Yawning and luxuriously stretching, she was quickly reminded of the exercise she and Marsh had indulged in during the night. She ached in very delicate places.

It felt amazing.

Pushing herself up, groaning at the pull in her thigh muscles as she slid her legs off the bed and stood up, Jen winced as she took a slow step.

Wow, she thought, moving slowly to the bathroom. She'd had no idea she'd hurt like this after reveling in so much unbelievable pleasure.

Can anyone say ecstasy?

Jen laughed softly at the wayward thought that swirled through her mind. But, in truth she had achieved ecstasy, or at least that was how she'd describe the shattering, mind-bending sensation Marsh had given her.

So she ached here and there…especially *there!* But oh, it was so worth it. Heaving a sigh of longing, Jen filled the tub with hot water.

She caught her breath as she slid into the tub, releasing it in relief when the heat of the water slowly began to ease the soreness from between her legs. Leaning back against the end of the tub Jen luxuriated until the heat dissipated. Then, draining the water, she stood and had a quick sluice down with warm water.

Forgoing makeup, she stepped into lacy panties and a matching bra. Wincing from a twinge of pain, she pulled on well-worn jeans, a cotton knit top and beaded-strap flip-flops.

Glancing around, Jen considered cleaning the apartment even though she had cleaned it Friday evening. She knew what she was doing, of course—marking time, looking for an excuse, *any* excuse, to stay inside the apartment and hide out.

Because Jen didn't want to face Marsh. What could she say to him? *Hey, you're a terrific lover, let's do it again sometime.* No, she most certainly couldn't say that, although that was the way of it. Even with her very limited knowledge she could tell he was an excellent and talented lover.

He apparently had plenty of experience.

She wondered if she'd passed the "compatibility test."

Jen sighed. Here she was, standing in the middle of her bedroom, dying for a cup of coffee and a big breakfast and afraid to go down the stairs and face him.

It was then that a shocking thought slammed into her mind.

Marsh hadn't used protection…and she had never had a reason to go on the pill.

What if…? Was it possible he had deliberately tried to impregnate her?

Jen mentally blocked the very idea, telling herself she wouldn't think of the possibility. Nevertheless, she did some quick mental tallying, relieved at the realization that it wasn't the right time of the month for conception.

Still, she knew the timing wasn't always reliable. She began to tremble. Should she run to a pharmacy for a morning-after pill?

Jen didn't run—she didn't even walk. She vacillated, uncertain, gnawing on her lip.

Oh, for pity's sake, move, she chided herself. *You're an adult woman, intelligent and strong. You can handle whatever fate throws at you. Now go get yourself a cup of coffee and something substantial to eat.*

But what if Marsh brought up the subject of marriage and babies again? What if that's all last night had been about for him?

Don't go looking for trouble, she told herself. *Deal with it if it comes looking for you.*

Squaring her shoulders, Jen left the room.

So her breathing was a trifle uneven, her heart rate a bit fast.

She'd live.

Marsh was in his office, sprawled lazily in his large butter-soft leather desk chair, the back of the seat facing the computer. His long legs were stretched out in front of him, crossed at the ankles, his feet bare. He had left the door open a few inches, waiting.

After the singular intensity of his release both times at the shattering climax with Jen, Marsh had almost immediately fallen into a deep sleep. Yet he had awakened less than four hours later, wanting more of her. She had been so tight and warm and…

Marsh felt certain Jen must be sore and aching. Only a brute would demand more, and he was no brute. His own body full, hurting with need, he'd slid her off his chest, chilled by the loss of her warmth, and settled her onto the mattress, tucking the comforter around her.

Scooping up his clothing he'd quietly left the apartment.

He had shaved, dressed, then went straight to his office, where he had been ever since. He hadn't eaten. His stomach was empty. He needed a gallon of coffee. He waited.

It was while he waited, aroused and ready, wanting her so bad it hurt, that memory stirred.

He had not protected her. Damn…and he had had

a package in his pocket, just in case he got lucky. And he had gotten very, very lucky. She was magnificent... and he hadn't protected her.

Marsh was unconcerned for himself. Truth to tell, he would love to have a child with her. But he hadn't deliberately left the condom in his pocket, not even subconsciously. He had too much pride to stoop to impregnating a woman in an attempt to bind her to him.

If it happened again—and he sure as hell hoped it did—he'd be sure to use protection.

Marsh didn't hear a sound, but he caught the scent of Jen when she reached the bottom of the stairs and headed for the kitchen. Exhaling a soft sigh of relief, he pushed himself out of the chair and followed her. Jennifer and coffee...what more could any man want?

"Coffee ready?"

Startled, Jen flipped the coffee scoop, sending the grounds flying to the floor.

"Good grief, Marsh!" she cried out, spinning around to glare at him, gasping for breath. "Are you trying to give me a heart attack?"

"I'm sorry." His lips twitched, making a lie of his apology. "I'll clean up the mess."

"You're damned right you will." She slammed her hands to her waist. "Meanwhile, can you be quiet long enough for me to make the coffee?"

"My lips are sealed," he said, turning away but not quickly enough to hide his smile from her.

Jen refilled the basket with fresh grounds and poured water into the pot. "Okay, the coffee will be ready in a few minutes." She turned back to him, raising her voice over the sound of the vacuum he was using to clean up the grounds. "Have you eaten?"

"No," he answered, shaking his head. "And I'm starving."

"Right," she drawled. "But then, when aren't you?"

Flipping the switch on the vacuum, he flashed a grin at her that caused a hitch in her breathing and a warm, exciting sensation in every cell and nerve in her body. "I can't deny it, I do love to eat."

"So do I," Jen admitted, proud of the steadiness of her voice when she was feeling overwhelmed with desire for Marsh—again. How much of this could she take? "So, what are you hungry for?"

Marsh ran a slow glance over her body. "Do you want the polite answer or the truth?" His voice was low, sensuous, suggestive.

"The polite answer," she quickly replied, fighting an urge to ask for the truth.

Marsh grinned. "Okay, then I'd like toast and a ham, cheese and tomato omelet, if you have the ingredients."

"I do." Telling herself to grow up and calm down, Jen headed for the fridge. "You can pour the coffee. I'm dying for a cup."

"Can't have that," he said, sounding amused. Opening the door on a cabinet he removed two large mugs and poured the coffee before the water had completely run through.

Ten minutes later they sat down to eat. Fifteen minutes after that they were both finished, not a crumb on their plates. Collecting the dishes, Jen stashed them in the dishwasher. She felt wonderfully full and nervous as hell. She had calmed down somewhat as she cooked and ate, but sitting back down at the table across from Marsh with nothing to occupy herself with but the coffee mug, the queasiness in her stomach started up all over again.

"So, what do you want to do today?"

The sensitized area between her thighs kept Jen from admitting to her desire to crawl back into bed with him and spend the rest of the day there. Instead, she said, "I'm going to finish the wash I started yesterday and then—"

"Don't even think about cleaning the house." Marsh cut her off in a warning tone.

Jen leveled a look at him. "If I had planned to clean the house, Mr. Grainger, I would clean the house," she retorted succinctly. "That's what I get paid to do."

"But I'm the boss, Ms. Dunning, and—"

"After the laundry," Jen said, figuring it was her turn to cut him off, "I'm going to curl up with the romance novel I started the night before last." Jen drew herself up, raised her chin and challenged his authority. "You got a problem with that?"

Marsh shrugged. "No," he said, his tone unconcerned. "It *is* your day off."

"Damn straight." She walked out of the kitchen and into the laundry room. The sound of his chuckle stalked her across the room, causing a hot shiver up her back to the nape of her neck.

"I'll be in my office," he said, then paused, his voice lowering to a sensual growl. "If you should need me for anything."

Oh, that's so not fair, Jen thought, digging out damp clothing and transferring it into the dryer.

Need him for anything? Jen's body began to heat up in very tender spots. Hell, she needed him for everything.

The very thought brought her to an absolute standstill. What on earth was she thinking? She didn't need anyone, least of all a man who was notorious for his disdain for women.

But Marsh really didn't seem like a man who disdained women. Did he? Or had he just worked his magic on her so completely that she couldn't tell what was real anymore?

Get a grip, she told herself.

Oh, sure, she had enjoyed her romp in bed with him—more than enjoyed it. She had reveled in it. It had been great sex. Well, she assumed it was great because it made her feel great. But that was no reason to lose her sense of reality.

Oh, hell, maybe it was time to take a hike, look for another job, maybe in another state, or even country, because she feared she was way out of her depth with Marshall Grainger.

But…she didn't want to leave. She loved her job. She loved—

No! Her stomach muscles twisted. It felt as if all her muscles twisted. Jen took off at a near run for her apartment.

"Jen?"

She stopped short on the fourth step, her breath catching in her throat at his soft call. "Yes?"

"Is something wrong?" He sounded concerned.

She half turned to look at him, immediately sorry she did so. He stood in the doorway to his office looking so blasted sexy. Somehow, Jen managed a reassuring smile.

"No, what could be wrong?" she asked, thinking, *Everything—everything could be wrong.*

He frowned. "Where are you going in such a hurry?"

How was it that even frowning he looked good enough to eat? She shook her head, trying to shake loose both the highly sexual image that flashed into her mind and the errant thought that went with it.

She inched backward and up one step. "I'm going to get my book. I decided to sit and read in the kitchen while waiting for the laundry to finish." *Liar, liar, pants on fire,* the tiny voice chided inside her head.

He smiled. She melted inside.

"The romance novel, right?"

"Yes."

"Is it good…the romance story?"

Jen grew stiff. Was there a note of mockery hidden inside his even tone?

"Yes, it is." She slid honey into her voice. "I wouldn't be reading it if it weren't." She raised one eyebrow. "What genre do you read?"

"I don't read fiction," he answered.

"Too bad, you don't know what you're missing."

"I'm a busy man, Jennifer. I have enough to read with business papers and periodicals."

"And what do you do to relax?" she asked, annoyed by his condescension.

This time his smile was slow, sexy, his eyes revealing his thoughts. "I was completely relaxed with you last night."

Jen froze, while the flame roared to life deep inside her. She didn't know what to say, how to respond to him. She certainly wasn't about to admit to the shimmering satisfaction he had given her. The last thing he needed was a booster shot to his ego.

He simply stood there, leaning against the door frame, his hands in his jeans pockets, his eyes hooded, his smile cool, for all appearances totally at ease.

Yeah, thought Jen, *like a tiger crouched and ready to spring.* Slowly, she backed up another step.

"I think we should get married." His remark startled Jen, even as something sprang to life inside her. She shouldn't have been surprised, of course—a part of her had known this was coming.

For a long moment the silence was complete. Then Jennifer erupted.

"You can't be serious, Marsh!"

"I am. You know I am."

Damn him. How could he be so calm when she felt about ready to fly into pieces? She stood there, shocked speechless, afraid that if she opened her mouth she'd admit the idea of spending every day and night with him for the rest of her life was very tempting.

Lazily, he straightened, moving away from the door, taking a step toward her.

Jen backed up another step.

He kept moving. "Getting married is the perfect solution."

"To what problem?" she asked, taking another step back, grasping the banister when she nearly stumbled.

She never saw him move but suddenly he was there, steadying her by drawing her into the safety of his arms.

"Are you okay?"

"Yes." She gulped air into her body. "I'm fine. You can let me go now."

"I'd rather not."

"Marsh, please." Jen drew another quick breath, which didn't help a bit in slowing her rapid heartbeat. "I need some time, some thinking space. We barely know each other, and certainly not well enough to get married."

"We have the rest of our lives to get to know each other," he said, his arms tightening possessively.

"Marsh, please, you're hurting me." It was a blatant

lie. While she *was* afraid, she wasn't afraid of him. What he was really doing was exciting her to the point where she feared she'd give him anything he asked of her.

"I've never deliberately hurt a woman in my life." His voice was now cold, his expression colder. His arms dropped away from her as he backed down the stairs to the foyer.

Reflexively, Jen reached out a hand, as if to stop his retreat. "Marsh, please." She wet her lips, shivering as she saw his narrowed eyes follow the path of her tongue. "It's too soon. I need time. As I told you before, it's been a long time since I've… Well, I've never experienced anything like what happened last night. It's a lot to process."

His cold expression shifted, giving way to warmth. "We do very well together, Jennifer." He smiled. "During the day *and* at night."

Jen bit her lip to keep from returning his smile. She was raking her mind for something coherent to say when he saved her from herself.

"Do you want to be courted?"

"Courted?" Jen blinked.

"Yes," he said, dead seriously. "You know, do things together besides sit across the table from each other at mealtimes."

"You mean like going riding and having dinner dates?" she asked.

"Sure, why not?" He smiled. "What do you enjoy doing in your free time besides reading?"

"You already know I like to ride." He nodded. "Well, I also like to play tennis and swim, and…" She grinned. "I like going shopping."

He gave her a wry look. "I'll ride with you. I'll play

tennis with you. I'll swim with you. We can go out to dinner, maybe even a movie now and again, but I draw the line at shopping."

She laughed. "Okay." She arched one brow. "But you'll still be the boss."

Smiling, he arched a brow right back at her. "During working hours, of course."

Jen nodded agreement. "Of course."

"But understand one thing, Jennifer," he went on, his voice now serious. "I fully intend to continue asking you to marry me until you say yes."

Jen froze. She should have known he was being too easy to get along with. Her silence must have warned him she was about to protest because he went still, too, his gaze hard on hers.

"I promise I won't force the issue."

"Okay," she said uncertainly.

"Now, promise you won't bolt to your car the minute I go into my office?" His voice was now a combination of suspicion and amusement.

Deciding the man was capable of driving a woman to drink—or dive straight into his arms—Jen nodded, lifted her hand to cross her heart with her forefinger and said, "I promise." She let a moment pass before adding, "I couldn't anyway. Most of my clothes are in your washer and dryer. But," she said as he turned to go, forcing him to turn back around, "I won't sleep with you at your beck and call." She hesitated a brief moment then added, "But I might, if I'm in the mood."

For a moment Marsh simply stared at her, then, surprising her, he agreed. "In that regard, you're the boss, and you'll call the shots."

Staring at him in wonder, Jen said, "Okay. Thank you."

"You're welcome. You know what?" He didn't wait for an answer. "You're cute when you're confused." Shaking his head he turned and walked back into his office, laughing. The echo of his bone-melting laughter lingered in her mind long after he had closed the door to his office.

Jennifer heaved a deep sigh. It simply wasn't fair for one man to be so damn attractive in so damn many ways. Of course, she knew she couldn't accept his proposal, such as it was. But it should be interesting to be "courted" by him.

Temptation whispered in the back of her mind: *grab him while his offer stands.*

Was she nuts? Possibly sharing his bed on occasion was one thing, but marriage? Shaking the very idea out of her head, Jen resumed climbing the stairs, and decided she'd stay upstairs—away from Marsh—for a while. Her heart was still pounding wildly and she wasn't quite sure she trusted herself around the man. She grabbed her book and sat, determined to keep any and all thoughts of Marsh from her mind by losing herself in the trials and tribulations of someone else's life for a while.

The story, a contemporary romance written by one of her favorite authors, immediately grabbed her attention. Within a few minutes, Jen's imagination slipped her into the role of heroine. It didn't take many pages, which Jen turned with increasing speed, before it became obvious the author was adeptly maneuvering the protagonists into a love scene.

What had started out with ever-increasing sensual banter quickly became heated. Without realizing it, Jen's body had grown taut, her breathing quick and shallow.

She turned a page and—

Her cell phone rang. Startled out of the hot and heavy scene, Jen muttered a curse and turned the book page down before answering the call.

"Jennifer, why haven't you come home for a visit, or at least called me?" Celia demanded imperiously.

At the sound of her mother's voice, an image flashed into Jen's mind of her mother in the throes of sex with a man who was not her husband. Would that awful image haunt her for the rest of her life? She dreaded the very idea.

Drawing a deep breath, she pushed the image aside. "I've been busy, Mother," she said, her voice a hair above a tremor. Her mother didn't seem to notice her distress. Of course, she thought, that was exactly like her mother.

"Surely you get weekends off," Celia snapped back. "He can't work you seven days a week."

He might try. Jen smiled at the very idea. "Of course not," she said. "This past weekend I drove to San Antonio to do some shopping."

"And last weekend and the weekend before that?" Celia's tone held a pout.

"Mother," she began, smothering an impatient sigh. That's as far as she got.

"Well, you absolutely must come home next weekend." Not a request, a command.

Indeed? Jen's eyebrows arched. "Why?" she asked, too politely.

"Don't you dare take that tone with me, Jennifer." Celia sounded on the verge of losing it. "The Terrells' Halloween masked ball is next Saturday, and as you are well aware, we always attend."

Oh, well then, why didn't you tell me at once? I

wouldn't dream of missing the Terrells' annual Halloween romp, Jen thought, her lips curling into a grimace. William Terrell—not Bill, never Bill, but always William—was the man in bed with her mother that awful night. His wife, Annette, was the woman with Jen's father.

"Mother, you know I have never cared for that party," she said, forcing herself to remain calm. "And I wasn't planning to attend this year. I'm not sure if I can make—"

"You will be here," her mother insisted. "For heaven's sake, Jen, all your friends will be there. They will be expecting to see you there, as well."

"Mother, I have been corresponding with my friends ever since I arrived here. I know for a fact that none of my gang is attending the party—they haven't in years," she said. "As a matter of fact, they feel as I do about it."

"And that is?" Celia asked.

"That we're past it. Our lives have gone in different directions. If you'll recall, the girls who always attend are no longer my friends. And they're still into the social scene. I've attended the Terrells' party because they are *your* closest friends." She nearly choked on the word *friends.*

"But—"

Jen quickly cut her off. "My true friends were never part of the social scene. All of us are into a different lifestyle." She gave a soft chuckle. "We work. We enjoy working."

"But if you come home, you would still be able to see them," Celia said. "I could arrange something."

Celia could be very convincing when she wanted to be. Even though Jen had kept in touch with her friends online, it was never the same as being in their company. It would be fun to see them. Until that moment, she didn't realize how very much she had been missing them.

And getting away from Marsh right now couldn't hurt, given the way he was making her feel. Which was, basically, turned on. Constantly. Which led her to think about dangerous things, like marrying him.

Going home for a visit would give her some serious thinking time.

"Okay," she capitulated, "but I won't stay long."

"Come for lunch," Celia said, adding before Jen could refuse, "I'll invite your 'gang,' as you insist on referring to them, to join us."

Jen made a face at the condescending inflection her mother had used with the word *gang*. Though she knew her mother held no animosity toward her friends, Celia still considered them beneath Jen. "What time?" she asked, suddenly tired and wanting the conversation to be over.

"Well," Celia now said with brisk satisfaction, "come early, but I'll invite the girls for one. Will that be all right with your schedule?"

"Yes, Mother." Jen gritted her teeth.

"Oh, and don't forget a costume." With that, her mother disconnected.

Great, Jen thought, resisting an urge to throw the phone across the room. A costume. She had forgotten the costume part of the stupid gala. She'd have to run into Dallas early, or possibly Friday evening, to pick up something suitable.

Maybe she'd go as a sexy vampire with long pointed teeth. That ought to make an impression.

The only question now was, how would Marsh react when she told him she was going home for a visit?

Or maybe the *real* question was, how would she feel being away from him for a few days?

She didn't like the answer she came up with...not one little bit.

Eight

Marsh began his courting campaign first thing on Monday morning, making Jen nervous before she'd even had her coffee.

Even at that early hour it was already warm outside and the weather forecast was for the temperature to rise into the eighties by the afternoon. After breakfast he said, "How about a game of tennis followed by a swim?"

Jen was struck dumb for an instant. Marsh always went directly to work after breakfast. She had never dreamed that this whole courting thing meant he'd actually take time out of his workday to spend with her.

"I'd love it," she said. "But we've got to—" That's as far as she got before he cut her off.

"We can work after we've had some exercise." Taking her hand, he led her away from the table. "Let's get changed." Releasing her, he sprinted up the stairs. "Last one on the court's a slowpoke."

"Hey, no fair," Jen protested as she chased after him.

To Jen's surprise, Marsh played a mean game of tennis. He won, but she made him work for it. "You're good," she said, bent over with her hands on her knees, drawing in deep breaths of air. "Where did you learn to play like that?"

Marsh was breathing every bit as heavily but he remained upright. "I was on the tennis team in college. You're good, too." He smiled at her. "For a few minutes there, I was afraid you'd beat me at my best sport."

Jen arched her brows in surprise. "You didn't play football?"

"Yeah, I did. But, after the first time I had my bell rung with a concussion I decided I liked tennis better." He flashed a killer grin at her. "My daddy didn't raise no fool."

From the court they went to the pool. Marsh stripped off his shirt and dove right in. Jen had pulled on a T-shirt and shorts over her bikini. Stepping out of the shorts and yanking the shirt off her sweaty body, she dove in after him.

There was no contest this time—they simply swam together. Jen was reveling in the sensation of the water rippling over her heated flesh when suddenly she let out a yelped, "Wha—!"

Marsh had dunked her.

Sputtering, Jen came up from the water to the sound of Marsh's laughter. She immediately retaliated. Jackknifing into a deep dive, she grasped his ankles and pulled his legs out from under him.

When he surfaced, Jen was laughing. For a moment, she watched him warily, but relaxed when he grinned at her.

"I deserved that," he admitted.

"Yes, you did," she said, grinning back at him.

"But I'll get you back for it," he teased. "Maybe not today, maybe not tomorrow, but I will get you back for it."

That night, to her surprise, Jen slept alone. As much as she told herself she was glad Marsh hadn't made as much as a suggestion that they share his bed, she didn't sleep well.

Dammit. Having decided she wouldn't sleep with him again until she was certain of his true feelings for her, she expected she'd feel relieved that he hadn't tried to seduce her. But all she felt was disappointment.

On Tuesday afternoon, Marsh left his office two hours earlier than usual and, rapping on Jen's door, ordered, "Pack it in, Jen, and go change into jeans and boots. We're going to ride into the sunset together."

Opening her office door, Jen gave him a wry look. "Ride into the sunset together?"

"Yeah, you've been buried every night in that romance novel," he said, grinning. "I thought asking you to ride into the sunset with me would sound romantic to you."

"You are a complete nut," she said, laughing at him.

"Maybe so," he drawled. "But I'm still the boss."

They actually did ride into the sunset. Standing side by side on the crest of a small hill, their mounts nibbling on the short grass nearby, Jen and Marsh watched the sun set the sky ablaze in breathtaking splashes of pink and streaks of lavender as it slowly disappeared in the distance.

"Romantic?"

Jen smiled at his hopeful tone. "Beautiful," she answered.

He took her hand, drawing her closer to him so he

could wrap his arm around her shoulders. "What about now?"

"Getting there," she murmured, drawing in the scent of him, the very essence of him.

Releasing her hand, he touched her cheek, drawing the tips of his fingers along her soft skin. She hitched a breath. At the soft sound, he lowered his head to brush his lips over her now trembling mouth.

"And now?" His breath teased her lips.

"Oh, yes." Raising her hand to the back of his head she brought his mouth to hers.

His kiss was sweet, gentle, wonderful for a full minute. Then, with a growl low in his throat, his desire took over.

Jen clung to him, owning him with her fierce embrace. Her feelings were running rampant. It was so good, so exciting, it was almost scary. Jen half expected Marsh to lower her to the grassy knoll, take her right there with the rainbow of colors arching across the twilight sky.

And she couldn't have stopped him.

But Cocoa and Star could.

Jen pulled away from Marsh when Star gave her a strong nudge against her shoulder. At the same time she heard Marsh curse as he was nudged by Cocoa.

"Unromantic beasts," he muttered, giving the horses a gentle shove away from them.

Jen couldn't control the burst of laughter that poured from her throat.

"Think it's funny, do you?" Marsh made a good attempt at a scowl, then lost it to his own roar of laughter.

"Yes, and so do you. And you were trying so hard, too."

"Trying?" One dark brow arched. *"Trying?"*

Leaning into him, Jen kissed his whisker-roughened cheek. "Actually, you were doing very well."

He reached for her. She danced away to grab up Star's reins. "Sunset's over. I think it's time to head back before it's dark."

"You don't need to be afraid of the dark," Marsh said, swinging up and into Cocoa's saddle as she mounted Star. "I'll protect you."

"I'll bet," she answered. "If I let you, you'll protect me right out of my jeans."

"Boy," Marsh said, in mock despair. "You are one very smart lady."

Jen laughed.

Marsh laughed with her.

By midweek, Jen could feel the changes occurring in their relationship. She was no longer wary of him, and she felt a closeness growing between them, a camaraderie.

And now he was approaching her about spending the night together, yet Jen held him off. No matter how often he complained of being lonely in that big bed of his, she stuck to her determination and slept in her own bed…alone, missing his closeness, his warmth.

As the days of the week slipped by, Jen knew she had to tell Marsh of her plans to drive to her parents' home in Dallas on Friday night. She had put it off, somehow knowing he wasn't going to be happy about her leaving. Thursday evening, Jen broached the subject after they had just finished a meal of salad and perfectly cooked steaks Marsh had made on the grill on the patio.

"Why?" he asked, when she had finished.

Why? Jen thought. "Why not?" she asked. They had spent most of the week together exclusively. Why shouldn't she spend one weekend away from him?

Marsh was getting to her—she was weakening toward his idea of them being together on a permanent basis. The realization was making her a bit edgy. Now, if he was going to start being possessive as well, she thought again that a little distance from him was a good idea.

Oh, who was she kidding? Jen was afraid she was falling for him, getting in too deep. So she took refuge in a show of independence.

She didn't even try to soften the impatience in her tone. "My weekends are free, aren't they?"

"Yes, of course." Marsh shook his head. "It just seems this came out of the blue. I was expecting to spend the weekend with you." His voice took on an edge, one she didn't particularly like. "Do you have plans or something?"

"Yes, I have plans," she said, surprised and annoyed by his manner. "On Saturday, I'm having lunch with several of my friends at my parents' home. And I'm attending the Terrells' party Saturday evening."

"Ah, the famous Terrells' Halloween masked ball, costumes required," he said in a ridiculing drawl, "and bedrooms available for couples for…private conversation."

That stopped Jen cold. "You're kidding," she said, raising an eyebrow. "Aren't you?"

Marsh smiled in superiority. "No, innocent one, I assure you, I am not kidding."

Jen wasn't sure what she resented more—his haughty smile or him calling her "innocent one." "But…"

"Have you been to the gala before?"

"Yes, I have, several times." Jen raised her chin in defiance. "Why do you ask?"

His silver eyes suddenly looked dark and stormy. "I

would have believed once would have been more than enough to turn you off the debauchery."

Debauchery? At the Terrells' party? She could believe it about the Terrells—she had seen them in action. Still, surely her old friends, who had also attended the gala for years, would have mentioned it. She was considering not attending the affair after all when Marsh decided the issue.

"I think you'd do better staying right here," he said, not quite an order but close enough.

"Then you can think again," she said, none too sweetly. "I'm going."

And that's when the cold front moved in.

They didn't speak to each other for the rest of the night. The next morning, while clearing away the dishes after a silent breakfast, Jen felt as if she was about to scream. Why was he acting like this? What did he expect she would do over the weekend—have a mad, wild fling with some mysterious man at the party? Is that why he had felt compelled to inform her—no, warn her—about the availability of bedrooms at the Terrells'?

Jen was building up a head of angry steam merely thinking about his manner. Without a word, she started walking out of the kitchen toward her office.

"Jennifer."

The snap in his tone stopped her cold. At the end of her patience, she whirled around to glare at him. "What?" Her tone had a decided bite.

"Go now," he said. "If you work the day, you'll have to drive to Dallas in the dark."

As if she hadn't known that, Jen thought. It was the end of October. Was he that eager to get her out of his sight? A pang zinged in her chest. *Fine,* she thought. *I'll give the man what he wants.*

She changed course from her office to the stairway.

Marsh came after her, coming to a stop one step below her. "Jen, wait," he said, his long fingers circling her wrist, his voice softening. "You are coming back, aren't you?"

Slowly turning, she gave him an arch look. "Well, I was planning on doing so, but if you keep snarling at me, I'll come back just to collect my stuff."

"Was I snarling?" While Marsh spoke, he was gently tugging on her wrist, slowly drawing her closer to him. "I realize I might have been a bit brusque, but snarling?"

His distinctive scent, his sheer maleness sent shivers rushing up her spine. Her heart began to thump, her breathing catch in her throat.

"Marsh," she managed to whisper when he raised her hand close to his face.

"I'm not going to hurt you," he murmured, lowering his head to touch his warm lips to her pounding pulse. "The last thing in this world I want to do is hurt you."

Jen's heartbeat seemed to stop altogether as his lips moved to the center of her palm. A warm sensation fluttered deep inside her. She had to get out of there, she thought, fighting an impulse to thread her fingers through his dark hair, lift his mouth to hers. If she didn't go now, at once, she'd be melting all over him, curling her arms around him, begging him to take her to his bed.

No, no, no. The word rang through her mind as she backed up a step, pulling her hands away from the temptation of his mouth, his body.

"Marsh, I'm going." Jen continued to back away, fighting her need for him every step of the way. To her relief—and also chagrin—he didn't follow her. But his gaze, a blaze of silvery-blue desire, tracked her every move.

"Have a good visit with your parents and your friends, Jennifer." His sensually soft voice stroked every nerve in her body. "And behave yourself."

Behave herself? Jen was suddenly fuming again. The man could make her crazy in an instant—it was amazing. Fortunately she had reached the landing as she spun to glare down at him, her nerves jangling now for an altogether different reason.

"I am not a child, Mr. Grainger," she said distinctly through gritted teeth. "And you will not speak to me as if I were. That is, if you would like me to come back."

He offered not an apology, as she had expected, but a blatantly sexy smile. "Oh, you'll come back, sweet Jen, because I know you want me as much as I want you."

Oh, hell, Jen thought. She did want him, dammit, here, now, right on the stairs. Shocked by how weak she was, how weak and needy he could so easily make her, she spun around and strode down the hallway to her apartment.

"Yes, you may go," he said, sounding more like a stern parent than an employer, never mind a lover.

"And you can go to hell, Marshall," she called back at him, slamming the door shut behind her.

Jen grabbed the carry-on she had packed that morning and turned to take a quick look at herself in the mirror. She hardly recognized the person looking back at her, a woman whose face was flushed with anger, frustration and more desire than she knew what to do with.

It was a good thing she was leaving for the weekend.

Opening the door just enough to peek out, Jen sighed her relief that Marsh was gone and dashed down to the garage. Tossing her stuff into the trunk, she jumped into the driver's seat and took off as though the devil himself was after her.

* * *

Why didn't I even say goodbye to her?

The question nagged at Marsh long after Jen's car had disappeared from view. Hell, it was less than an hour since she had driven away and already he was missing her. He was missing everything about her.

If he was honest with himself, Marsh knew damn well why he hadn't carried her bag and walked her to her car like a gentleman. He was sulking like a spoiled kid because he hadn't had his own way.

Still, he admired her for defying him. He admired her for everything she was—tough, unafraid and soft and sweet...at times.

This was the second time he'd managed to drive her away. What was he doing wrong? Marsh wasn't used to getting things wrong with women. He was used to his words and actions always having the desired effect, and to getting exactly what he wanted. But with Jen, it was completely different. There was something about her, something about the way she saw him—she didn't automatically do or say what he wanted. She thought for herself, and wasn't instantly swayed by whatever charm he was laying on.

As annoying as that was, it was also hotter than hell.

The days they had spent together "courting" were some of the best of his entire life. Besides her ability to stand on her own two feet, what was it about her that had so captured his interest and imagination?

She intrigued him. She was *more* than any other woman he had ever met—he didn't know how else to say it. And since Marsh couldn't explain it to himself, he'd never consider even trying to explain his feelings to anyone else.

Especially not to her.

He wanted her, wanted her more than any other woman he had ever met. He wanted her until he ached with the wanting, ached in his body and mind. But it was about more than that. It wasn't just the mind-blowing sex, it was…what?

It was nuts. That's what it was. It was totally and completely nuts. But there it was. As badly as he wanted to be a father, to have an heir, he *needed* more. He wanted her—and only her—to be the mother of his children.

The realization shocked him. It wasn't just that he wanted her to accept his business proposition so he could have what he wanted. It was that he wanted to build something with her, he wanted her by his side, he wanted her to be his partner in life.

He wanted…a life. With her. Period.

So what the hell was he supposed to do now?

At lunchtime, Jen stopped at a roadside pizza shop. Sitting in a booth at the window, she sipped iced tea as she glanced at the strip mall on the other side of the highway. Checking out the stores, her glance passed, then returned, to the second to last of them.

Holidays, Holidays, Holidays arched across the display window, which was decorated with everything Halloween.

Less than a half hour later, Jen parked the car in the lot close to the store. She was pleased to discover that the merchandise was of a much better quality than usually found in discount stores. After all, she couldn't show up at the gala in a cheap costume—her mother wouldn't hear of it.

"Need help?" a smiling woman asked from behind a cash register. "Or just browsing?"

Jen returned her smile. "I don't think I need help, just directions to the costumes."

The woman waved her arm. "They're along the back wall. That's what's left of them."

"Thanks," Jen said. "I'll have a look."

The woman hadn't been kidding—what was left on the wall was slim pickings. Still, one costume hanging near the end caught her eye at once.

"Perfect," she murmured, coming to a halt in front of a gypsy-girl outfit. She touched the full black skirt shot through with golden thread. *Velvet?* Jen thought, surprised. Her hand moved from the skirt to the off-the-shoulder loose blouse. *Silk?* Amazing. The garment was a deep red, the neckline and long sleeves trimmed with a wide ruffle.

Carmen. The name jumped into her head along with an image of the outfit worn by the sultry soprano who had performed the role of the lusty Carmen when Jen had attended the opera at the Met the last time she had visited New York City.

She called out to the clerk to join her at the back.

"Find something, did you?" the woman asked, coming to a stop next to Jen, her gaze drifting to the costume. "Beautiful, isn't it."

Jen nodded. "Gorgeous."

"A bit pricey," the woman added, as if in warning.

"That's all right," Jen said. "I'm going to need a few accessories."

"I've got it covered. Come with me."

When Jen left the store, she was carrying a shopping bag in each hand, a small smile of satisfaction curving her lips. The skirt, blouse and accessories had cost her a bundle but she didn't care. Since learning the truth about her parents' indiscretions with the Terrells, she had decided this was the last Terrell Halloween bash she would ever attend. This was the last time she was ever going to appease her mother in this regard, so she might as well go all the way.

When she got home, she was struck by a strange sensation. After only a few weeks away, the word *home* didn't seem to fit anymore. When, she wondered, had she begun thinking of Marsh's place as home?

Jen realized she had started to consider his place her home after the incredible night they had spent together. The fact that the atmosphere around the house had felt strained since their argument didn't matter—it still felt like home. And that fact alone was kind of scary.

After parking her car in the slot that had been hers ever since she got her driver's license when she was seventeen, Jen entered the house by the kitchen door.

She had spent many hours in the kitchen while she was growing up, warmly welcomed there by Tony. She had learned her cooking skills from him in that kitchen…the skills Marsh so vocally appreciated.

Marsh.

Jen sighed. She had been gone less than a day and she was homesick. She scolded herself, heading for the elevator in the hallway right off the kitchen. The elevator rose to her apartment, which took up the entire second floor of the wing attached to the house. Her father had built the wing to house Jen's grandmother when the elderly woman's arthritis put her in a wheelchair.

Jen had adored her grandmother, who died while Jen was in her junior year of college. After graduation Jen had moved into the apartment, and even though she had replaced the Victorian-style furniture and decorations the older woman favored with more modern things, she still felt close to her grandmother there.

That was before she went to live in Marshall
Grainger's sprawling house. Stepping inside the living
room Jen had once felt so comfortable in, she set her
shopping bags on the floor and sighed as she dropped
into her favorite chair.

The roomy place now seemed no more welcoming
than an expensive hotel suite.

It wasn't the house in the hill country she was missing, Jen reluctantly admitted to herself. It was the man
living in it, waiting for her return.

Oh, Lord, I am in trouble, Jen thought. *Willingly or
not, I have fallen in love with Marshall Grainger.*

The man who had not so much proposed to her as
decided all on his own that they should get married.

For business reasons, essentially.

This was the man she'd decided to fall in love with?

She heaved a heavy sigh. If only he had indicated
some genuine feelings for her. Oh, he enjoyed her company, liked teasing her, kissing her, touching her and
pursuing more intimate, sensual, exciting endeavors.
And while she reveled in his attention, and couldn't
believe the extreme pleasure he was able to give her
over and over again, she still longed for him to confess deeper feelings for her. But he never did, and she
feared he never would.

Arrogant jerk.

Calling him names in silent frustration didn't help
at all, she found.

She was still in love with him.

Sighing, Jen shook her head, as if shaking thoughts
of Marsh from her mind—yeah, right—and rose to
scoop up the bags to carry to her bedroom.

Before getting settled, she decided she had better let
her mother know she was back. Lifting the phone from

her nightstand, Jen hit the button for the interior of the house. Ida, the housekeeper for as long as Jen could remember, answered with the first buzz.

"Yes?"

"Hi, Ida," Jen greeted the woman warmly. "It's Jen. Is Mother there?"

"Hi, honey," the older woman replied, still using the same endearment she had always used with Jen. "No, your mother had a dental appointment this afternoon. Are you hungry?"

Jen laughed. Those words had always been the first thing Ida had asked her whenever she walked into the house. "Well, come to think of it, I could eat a snack. I haven't eaten since lunch and all I had was a slice of pizza. What are you offering?" Frowning she tacked on, "Where is Tony? I came in through the kitchen and it was empty."

"He went grocery shopping," Ida said, amusement in her voice. "He wanted some special goodies to serve you and your friends for lunch tomorrow."

"Oh, I can hardly wait," Jen said.

Ida laughed again. "Well, would you settle for a cold roast beef and cheese sandwich now?"

"Hmm, sounds good. Give me a few minutes and I'll be down."

"Take your time."

It took only minutes to hang up the skirt and blouse Jen had purchased. Leaving the apartment, she strode to the end of the hallway and clattered down the back stairs.

"Jennifer's home," Ida said, laughing as Jen entered the room. "Do you ever *walk* down a flight of stairs, honey?"

"Only when I'm being a lady, which isn't too often,"

Jen answered, walking to the woman and right into her arms. "It's good to see you, Ida."

"Oh, Jennifer," Ida said, "I miss you—your laughter, your bounding up and down stairs."

"I miss you, too." Stepping back, she sighed. "I had to go. I needed new…scenery."

Ida nodded. "I understand."

Jen suspected Ida knew and understood everything that ever happened in this house. "I know you do," she replied, lowering her gaze.

"Now, then," Ida said briskly. "Your sandwich is ready and I have a fresh pot of coffee brewing."

"You know me so well." Crossing the room to the large solid wood table, Jen seated herself in front of the plated sandwich with a pickle slice next to it.

Tony came in the back door toting two canvas grocery bags just as she was finishing the sandwich. Without much coaxing, she soon had him and Ida at the table with her, the three of them drinking coffee and chatting away, catching up with one another.

Ida had left the kitchen to go finish up what she had been doing when Jen buzzed her, Tony was in the pantry and Jen was nursing her second cup of coffee when her mother swept into the room.

"There you are," she said with a note of censure, as if Jen had no business in the kitchen.

"Yes, here I am," Jen said, rising to accept the brief hug and air-kiss her mother brushed over her cheek. "How are you, Mother?"

"I'm fine now that the dentist has taken care of the tooth that was bothering me." Her gaze touched on the cup on the table. "Is there any coffee left?"

"Yes, I'll get some for you." Scooping up her cup,

Jen went to the cabinet, took out another cup, then filled both with the aromatic brew. Tony bought only the best.

Sitting close to her mother while they sipped their coffee was a novel experience for Jen—they had never done it before. *Why now, after all this time?* Jen wondered as she glanced at her mother, struck by how odd it was to sit with her in the kitchen.

"I wasn't expecting you until tomorrow." Her mother's eyebrows rose in question.

"I left this morning. Mr. Grainger gave me the day off."

Her mother nodded but didn't say anything about Marsh, even though Jen had expected she would. "Did you get a costume or must you still go shopping?"

"I got one. I stopped for lunch and noticed a holiday shop in a strip mall across the highway. There wasn't a large selection left but I found one."

"Are you going to tell me what it is?" her mother asked.

Jen shrugged. "It's only a gypsy outfit," she answered. "But as I said, the selection was small."

"I think a gypsy outfit will do fine."

Jen hid the smile tickling her lips. Her mother was in for a shock when she saw what Jen was going to do with the outfit. "What's your costume?"

"I'm going as a Southern lady in an antebellum costume."

What else? Jen thought. "I bet it's gorgeous. I can't wait to see it. I presume Dad's wearing the costume of the Southern gentleman?"

"Yes, of course," she answered.

Rhett Butler, of course. Jen smiled. Her parents would be a spectacular couple. Jen enjoyed the thought for a moment, until she heard Marsh's words ringing in her ears about the bedrooms at the masked ball. She looked away from her mother for a moment, trying to bring herself back to the present.

Her mother finished her coffee and walked to the sink to rinse her cup. "I'm afraid you'll be alone for dinner, Jennifer," she said. "As we weren't expecting you until tomorrow, your father and I accepted a dinner engagement for this evening."

"That's all right, Mother," Jen said. "I'm sure I can find a crust of bread and a bit of cheese to eat."

"I beg your pardon?" Tony scowled at her from the doorway to the pantry.

Jen laughed. Her mother even managed a chuckle. "I'm off to have a short nap." She again brushed Jen's cheek, this time with a real and surprising kiss. Celia hesitated a moment then murmured, "If you'll follow me, I'd like for us to have a talk before I take my nap."

Jen blinked before nodding her head. "I'll be up in a minute."

Without another word, her mother swept from the room.

"She certainly knows how to make an entrance and exit," Tony drawled as he strolled into the room. "And you, young lady, you will enjoy a delicious dinner right here in the kitchen." He tried to look angry, which was pretty funny.

"On one condition." Jen scowled back at him.

"Name it." He cocked an eyebrow.

"You and Ida join me at the table."

He smirked. "I was planning on it."

Curious about her mother's startling request for a discussion—and it was a request, not an order—Jen went straight to her mother's lavishly decorated bedroom. And it *was* her mother's bedroom. Celia and John had slept in separate bedrooms for as long as Jen could remember.

She lightly knocked on the wood panel, softly calling, "Mother?"

The door immediately swung inward, almost as if her mother had been hovering on the other side, anxiously waiting for her daughter.

"Come in, dear," she said, indicating a small table flanked by two chairs. "Have a seat."

"Thank you," Jen said, inwardly frowning at the puzzling invitation as she sat.

"Jennifer," Celia said, seating herself in the other chair, "I think it's time for you and I to have a mother-and-daughter, heart-to-heart talk."

Stunned, Jen stared at her mother. "A heart to heart?" she repeated. "Mother, isn't it a little late for that? I'm crowding thirty. I know all about the birds and the bees. Men and women, too," she said, attempting to make a joke to break the tension. What on earth was her mother about to say?

"I know, dear." Celia's smile was sad. "I wasn't referring to you. I was referring to me." She paused, and swallowed. "To me, and William Terrell."

"Mother, I…" Her voice came out raw. Not wanting to hear whatever her mother had to tell her, Jen put her hands on the arms of the chair to stand. She practically wanted to run from the room.

"Jennifer, listen." Celia placed a hand on Jen's arm, keeping her seated. "I need to explain the situation."

Jen tried once again to rise. This time her mother stopped her with the desperate plea in her voice.

"Jennifer, please."

Cringing inside, Jen sank back into the chair, half-sick about what she feared she was going to hear. "Okay, Mother, I'll listen."

Celia drew a deep breath before saying, "You saw us together at some point, didn't you?" She asked the question as if certain Jen would know what she meant by "together."

"Yes." It was barely a whisper from Jen's trembling lips. "And Dad with Annette." She drew a quick breath. "I left my car out front and came up the stairs heading for my place." Tears were trembling on the edges of her eyelids. "The doors were open and…"

"That's enough." Celia sounded choked, her elegant fingers squeezing her daughter's arm.

Jen sent a quick glance at her mother, a pang twisting in her chest at the sight of tears running down her mother's beautiful face. She wanted to run, yet she couldn't move, her knees weak, her body trembling.

"Will you listen as I explain?" The strain in Celia's voice caused another pang in Jen's chest.

Afraid to trust her own voice, Jen nodded her assent.

"I love your father but I'm not in love with him." She sighed. "I've known him all my life. Our families were neighbors. He and I grew up together. I was always trailing after him. For some time, he tried to chase me away," she said, a smile touching her lips, "but eventually he gave in and let me follow him around. We were companions, pals." Here, her voice hardened. "We were never romantically interested in each other."

"But then—" Jen was silenced by her mother's raised hand.

She drew another deep breath before continuing. "Unknown to either your father or me, soon after my birth, our parents decided it would be a perfect idea to betroth the two of us, thereby keeping the wealth of the families together."

Jen simply could no longer be quiet. Eyes widening in disbelief, she said, "That is absolutely ridiculous."

"Yes, of course it is," Celia agreed, shaking her head. "Let me finish the entire stupidity of it all, then you can say anything you wish." She raised her brows. "Okay?"

"Okay." Jen sank back into the padded chair. But she managed to add, "I suppose we should have just had our coffee up here."

Celia gave a soft laugh. "I suppose we should have, but we can do that another time."

Realizing her mother was offering a sort of olive branch, Jen felt another sting of tears in her eyes. Indelicately sniffing, she said, "I'd like that."

"And I." Her smile wider now, Celia brushed the tears from her cheeks before continuing. "At the time our respective parents informed us we were getting married, neither your father nor I had met anyone we were romantically interested in, although we had both dated others. Of course, there was one holdout—your grandmother. She adored her son, and she liked me. She didn't think it was fair to either of us."

"She was right," Jen said.

"Yes—" Celia nodded "—but she was overruled. Both of us caved in to their demands." She closed her eyes as if in pain. "Praying we could come to fall in love, we really tried. We were both delighted when I realized I was pregnant with you, and thrilled when you were born."

Sniffling, Jen nodded.

Celia handed her a small box of tissues, taking one herself. After mopping up, she went on with her story.

"Then I met William." She briefly closed her eyes.

When she opened them she stared straight into Jen's. "I fell in love with him at first sight, and he with me." She paused to give Jen time to respond if she wanted to do so.

Jen remained quiet, waiting until her mother finished.

"I give you my word of honor, Jennifer, nothing happened between William and me until two years later." She shook her head as tears started once more. "That was when your father and Annette told William and me that they were in love." She shook her head in despair. "Sorry tale, isn't it."

Jen couldn't remain seated—she jumped to her feet. "Why didn't you get divorced?" she cried. "Hasn't it been hell living like this?"

"Of course it has, and we did discuss the possibility of divorce," Celia said, getting up to face Jen. "But by then your father's family's finances were so entwined with my family's, and there was you and the Terrells' son, Bill Jr., to consider." She dropped back onto the chair as if exhausted. "We decided to go on as we have been." She swiped at the tears with a delicate hand.

Trembling, shoulders shaking, not knowing exactly what she was feeling about the whole mess, Jen sat back down on the edge of the chair and covered her eyes with her hand.

"Jennifer, please try to understand. I love your father. We are still companions and pals. He feels the same, but there's William and Annette…" Sighing, she let her voice trail away.

"Mother," Jen began, anxious about the defeated look on Celia's face.

"I've wanted to talk to you so often, to bare my soul, but you seemed to always be running away, if only to hide inside yourself." Her soft voice was tinged with pain, her eyes wet again. "Can you ever forgive us, Jennifer?"

"There is nothing to forgive, Mother," she said, walking the few steps needed to wrap her arms around her mother. "This is your life—yours and Dad's." Stepping back, she gave her mother an understanding smile.

Now Celia was sniffling. She laughed as Jen handed her a tissue before taking one herself.

"Will you talk to Dad, tell him I'm not angry or resentful? I'm not, you know. I'm just glad you explained it to me."

Celia sniffed once more. "We do love you very much, you know. We always have. And we are very proud of you."

"Thank you." Jen echoed her mother's sniff. "I love you, too." Jen smiled and turned to leave the room. "Now I'm going to get out of here and let you get your nap. It wouldn't do to have you go out tonight looking tired and puffy-eyed, and not like your usual lovely self."

As she opened the door Celia said softly, "Thank you, Jennifer. Have a nice dinner with the help."

Startled, Jen glanced back in time to see her elegant mother give her a wink. Laughter bubbling up inside her, she closed the door.

But when she was back in her apartment, Jen had to sit down and take a moment for herself. An arranged marriage. Her parents had an arranged marriage. She could barely wrap her mind around it. While it helped her to understand what was going on between them, it was strange to know that she was the product of a union between two people who were not in love, and never had been.

Jen moved to the queen bed in her bedroom, intending only to rest for a while, to give her mind the time to process all that she had learned. Suddenly, an image of Marsh came to mind, and she shivered, realizing the similarity between Marsh's proposal and the marriage her parents shared. She closed her eyes against the sudden sting of hot tears. She couldn't—absolutely could not stand it if, having agreed to marry him, Marsh later met and fell deeply in love with another woman. She didn't think her heart could take that. But wasn't that what would happen, if she entered into an arranged marriage of sorts with Marsh? If he wasn't in love with her, he certainly wouldn't stay with her if he fell in love with someone else. A man like Marsh had opportunities all the time—it wouldn't take much for him to accept one.

Jen knew right then and there that she couldn't continue to work for Marsh, to live with him…to be with him. It was too dangerous for her heart. She would go back to the house after the Terrells' party and hand him her notice in answer to his proposal.

Running away again? The thought drifted through her tired mind. She didn't run from life—did she?

Actually feeling sick to her stomach, she banished the thought for a few moments of calming meditation. She created a beach scene in her mind, wavelets rippling upon the sand. And a woman, hands jammed into the pockets of a jacket, head down, walking down the beach…alone. Tears streaming, Jen finally drifted off to sleep.

Leaving his workout room on the second level of the garage, Marsh was covered with sweat. Frustrated by what he thought of as Jennifer's defection after the incredible times they had shared the previous few days, he had tried to work out his simmering anger by punching the hell out of the big bag hanging from the ceiling.

When that didn't work, he followed up by running like a fighter in training on the treadmill.

That didn't work, either.

In fact, it hadn't helped much at all except to make him sweaty and tired. After a shower, Marsh pulled on jeans and a T-shirt and walked barefoot down the stairs to his office, only to stare sightlessly at the cursor on his computer screen.

She hadn't called since she'd left. He couldn't believe that he'd been waiting to hear from her, but he had. Marsh had never, ever in his entire life "sat by the phone," so to speak, waiting for a woman to call him. He just wasn't that type of man.

Or at least, he hadn't been…until he'd met Jen.

He missed her, more than he had believed himself capable of missing any woman. *I want a life with her* kept ringing through his head. He had never had that thought about anyone before, not even the woman he had married.

Damn, why had he let Jen go to Dallas?

Marsh snorted aloud at himself. How could he have stopped her? By taking her to bed? While the idea held appeal—a lot of appeal—Marsh knew that Jen would have resented him for using sex to keep her there. And she probably would have left afterward anyway.

Just the thought of sex with Jen made Marsh crazy with longing. He shifted on his leather desk chair to relieve the ache in the lower part of his body. Images of her beautiful naked body ran through his head and he was powerless to stop them. Her incredible eyes, her perfect breasts, her flat stomach, the sweetness between her long legs…

He needed her. It was a very difficult admission for him to make, even to himself. But he wanted her. And despite the fact that he'd gotten hard just thinking about her, he didn't just want her naked in his bed. He wanted her here in the house, in the swimming pool, riding horses over his land, cooking with him on the patio grill, softly singing while she went about her work. A shadow of a smile feathered his lips as he wondered if she hummed while working in her office.

"Oh, hell." Marsh gave up and, bending to the trash basket beside his desk, picked out a silver-trimmed black card. The printing on the card was bloodred, requesting his company at the Terrells' Annual Halloween Ball. He had, as usual, received the invitation weeks ago, even though he not only never attended, he didn't even bother to respond.

Sighing in defeat, Marsh put his computer to sleep, pushed back his chair and strode from his office to the stairs.

If you can't fight 'em, join 'em, he thought.

Hell, he'd have to find a costume. The very idea of him, Marshall Grainger, putting on a stupid costume for a woman, was a hard truth to swallow.

But then an idea struck him in a flash. It was easy enough to pull off. And the best part was, he had almost everything he needed right in his apartment in Dallas.

A few hours later, Marsh was exceeding the speed limit as he headed for the city. He caught sight of the perfect shop only because he had to stop for a red light—Holidays, Holidays, Holidays, it was called. Making a quick turn when the light turned green, he parked and strode into the shop and found what he needed to complete his outfit.

Marsh grimaced as he tossed his store bag into the

car. He detested getting dressed in a stupid costume, even if it was the simplest disguise he could come up with. He shook his head and slipped behind the wheel.

The lengths a man will go to just to get a woman into his bed...permanently.

Nine

The phone on Jen's bedside cabinet buzzed, waking her from her nap. Yawning, she picked up the receiver. "Yes?" she asked, still only half-awake.

"Good morning, glory, did you see the rain...dear?" Tony's chipper voice sang in her ear.

Jen laughed. "You're a goof, and it's not morning and it's not raining."

"I know, but her majesty has left the building and supper is ready, so rustle your tush down here."

"Give me five minutes," she said.

"Okay, princess, see you in five." He disconnected.

Jen didn't move for a moment, as the conversation she had had with her mother came rushing back to her. She pondered the situation for a minute, reminding herself that her parents' lives were their business. And Celia's heartfelt avowal of their love for her eased a hurt that Jen had buried deep inside herself.

But she still couldn't help thinking about how her parents' situation compared to her situation with Marsh. She knew what she had to do. She hated it, but she knew it.

She set the phone aside and went to her bathroom to splash water on her face before brushing her teeth. Exactly four and a half minutes later she ran into the kitchen announcing, "I'm here and I'm starving. What's for supper?"

"One of your favorites," Tony announced. "Cheese-burgers and Greek salad," he finished.

"Oh, heavenly," she said, running around the table to hug him. "You whip up the best Greek salad in the whole world."

"I know." Tony grinned back at her.

Ida stood patiently behind her chair at the table, smiling indulgently. "If you two are done with your comedy act?" she said dryly.

Tony gave Jen a quick hug before stepping back from her embrace. "You see, Jennifer, that's the reason I don't marry her. I hear nothing but nag, nag, nag."

"Oh, I see," Ida shot back, primly seating herself at the table. "I'm good enough to sleep with but not to marry."

"Ida!" Tony glanced at Jen in alarm. "Cover your ears."

"I'm a big girl, Tony, and I've known about you and Ida for years now."

Tony appeared half-sick. "How did you find out?"

"For heaven's sake, Tony," Ida chided him. "I told her."

Tony brought a hand up to his chest as if in pain. "I can't stand it," he cried dramatically as he set a luncheon plate in front of Jen. "Anyway," he groused, "I did ask her to marry me, at least a hundred times. She said no."

Jen shot a startled look at Ida.

The older woman shrugged. "Why ruin a great relationship?"

Curious and surprised by the older woman's attitude, Jen decided to keep her opinion to herself.

Later, back in her room, Jen pondered the exchange between Tony and Ida. They were close to the same age, somewhere in their late fifties, Jen figured. They made an odd couple. Ida was of medium height, a bit plump and still very pretty, her face unlined. She had lost her husband to cancer after only a few years of marriage and apparently didn't feel the need to marry again. So she had made a home with Jen's parents.

Tony was flat-out handsome, tall and lean with gleaming dark eyes and a ready smile. And he was one terrific cook. Jen had often wondered why he had never opened his own restaurant. Now she wondered if he stayed with her parents to be with Ida.

While they both had their own quarters in the huge house, Jen knew they slept together in Tony's bed.

Is that what Marsh had in mind for her? The thought wormed its way into her mind, making her restless. Getting out of her chair, Jen began to pace the apartment as if by walking she could find the answers to her dilemma.

Marsh had said he wanted marriage and children.

Without love.

Jen shivered at the chill that snaked down her spine. Whereas Ida and Tony had love without marriage, Jen found herself facing the idea of marriage without love, just like her parents. She couldn't help thinking that Ida had the best deal.

Like other young women, Jen had wanted marriage and children. But she had always dreamed that love would come first. And while she admittedly was head-over-heels in love with Marsh, he was admittedly hot for her body.

Although he did consider her good wife and mother material. But so what? What good was any of that without love?

Sighing, Jen looked around, finding herself in her bedroom. She plopped onto the bed to be comfortable while ruminating.

Fat chance of being comfortable while thinking about Marshall Grainger.

What to do? Was it enough that she loved him? Should she take a gamble and marry Marsh even though she knew he didn't love her? Should she accept his offer—be his wife, keep his books, take care of his home, cook his meals and share his bed and someday, hopefully, bear his children?

Jen felt a twist of longing inside. She so wanted to bear his children…their children.

She was already keeping his home and his books and cooking his meals. Why not take the next leap of faith and pray they could make a go of marriage, even if he didn't love her? They would have the intimacy of the bedroom, and in truth Jen craved his body as much as he seemed to crave hers.

Was that enough for her? Could she make it enough? Was she strong enough to live out her life under those conditions? Jen bit her lower lip. Like a greedy child she wanted it all—all of Marsh, including his love.

But, she reminded herself, Marsh didn't believe in love.

Square one.

This was real life, Jen told herself, heaving a deep sigh. She loved him, and was beginning to doubt that she would ever love any other man. In real life one played the hand that was dealt—it was pointless to wish for it all. That was the stuff of romantic fairy tales, dreamed by teenagers.

She was a woman, a woman in love with a man who wasn't going to love her back.

And it sucked.

Jen woke the next morning still balanced on the sword of indecision, so to speak. Although she had gone to bed early, she had lain awake most of the night mentally replaying the pros and cons of her present situation.

All things considered, Jen simply could not decide what to do about her relationship with Marsh. She had changed her mind several times already, going from vowing never to see him again to agreeing to marry him. Teetering on the edge was not her style, as a rule. For just about as long as she could recall, Jen had thought through a problem then quickly made a decision, as she had when deciding to accept Marsh's terms of employment.

On reflection, Jen thought what she should have done at the time was jump back into her car and run. Then, having only just met him, she could have gone on her way, personally unaffected by him…except for that strange sizzling sensation that zinged up her arm when they first shook hands.

It had started right away. She should have fled when she still had the strength.

She replayed her conversation with her mother, in which her mother said she was always running away in some way, shape or form. She frowned. Had she been running away her whole life, first from the guy in the school parking lot? Had she run to the hill country after finding her parents in compromising positions with their best friends?

Had she run back to Dallas to escape her feelings for Marsh?

Jen shook her head to dispel the vision in her mind, only to find herself with her thoughts of Marsh again. In time, the memory of his touch would pass, wouldn't it? Gazing at her hand, Jen had an eerie sensation she could still feel him. Maybe the sensation wouldn't have passed.

Somehow she knew she would very likely never forget those delicious sensations.

She got out of bed and headed into the bathroom for a shower. She had to shove thoughts of Marsh aside and pull her act together. Her friends were due to arrive for lunch in less than an hour.

She set the shower at full blast hoping the cold water would clear her thoughts. Maybe time with her "gang" could help her decide what to do about the new man in her life.

It was time to come clean with them about where she'd been all this time—and who she'd been with.

Her friends were right on time, all five—Kathie, Marcie, Karen, Leslie and Mary—pulling their cars into the driveway one after the other. Jen ran to meet them.

After hugs all around, they made their way into the house. The grilling started almost immediately.

"All right, Jen, where did you run off to?" Kathie demanded, giving Jen a mock stern look.

"I missed you!" Marcie said, putting on a pout.

"Yeah, you sneak, it's time to come clean," Karen added.

"If you'll recall," Jen chided, herding them into the house, "I kept in touch online."

"But you said absolutely nothing," Mary replied.

"There's a man, isn't there?" Leslie asked.

Jen ushered them through the dining room and onto the shaded patio where Tony had laid an elegant setting for seven on the round garden table. Glasses of iced tea were waiting for them.

It was a perfect day for lunch outside. The temperature was in the high seventies with a lovely fall breeze. "Isn't it gorgeous out?" Jen asked.

"Come clean, Jen, *now*." It was an order from Kathie in her sternest drill-sergeant tones.

"Who are you working for? More to the point, what kind of work are you doing? And why did you leave so mysteriously?" Marcie asked.

"I'm getting suspicious," Mary said, giving her a narrow-eyed look.

"And I'm getting impatient," Karen added.

Jen held her hand up to get them to stop. "I'll tell you all about him—about everything. Let's just sit down first, okay?"

"Is he deliciously handsome and sexy?" The salacious note Leslie had managed to achieve had all of them laughing as they settled at the table. It was like old times, the six of them laughing together as they so often had in college. It was wonderful—just the tonic Jen had been needing.

The laughter came to an abrupt stop when Jen's mother joined them at the table. Seating herself, she glanced around the table, one eyebrow arched.

"Having fun, ladies?"

"Actually, we were, Mother," Jen said. "It was as if we were back in the dorm again."

"We're trying to get your daughter to tell us who she's working for," Karen asked.

"For whom, dear," her mother corrected. "You don't know about Jennifer and Marshall Grainger?" Now both eyebrows were raised.

Jen nearly spit out her drink.

"Marshall Grainger?" Kathie repeated in awed tones.

"Holy…shoot," a wide-eyed Marcie said, catching herself to clean up her language just in time.

All the women at the table looked at Jen, waiting for her to offer some sort of explanation.

"Yummy," Leslie said. "But Marsh Grainger isn't exactly—"

"How did you even—" began Kathie.

"It's a long story. I swear, I'll tell you everything. Later," Jen added.

"Well, this is a happy group, isn't it?" Tony drawled, coming to a halt at the table. "Shall I wait a few minutes to serve?"

"Heck no, I'm starving," Marcie said.

Only Marcie, Jen thought fondly. "No, you can serve now, please," Jen said.

"May," her mother corrected again. "You *may* serve now, Tony, thank you."

Who, whom, can, may—what the hell difference did it make? She was among friends, her very best friends. Though Jen was sorely tempted to say something very impolite to her mother, she held it back, not wanting to spoil her friends' good humor and lunch. Besides, she didn't want to endanger the accord she and her mother had reached yesterday afternoon.

Tony had prepared a wonderful warm day luncheon.

In the center of the table he set a large pitcher of freshly brewed iced tea with mint. "There's more of everything, ladies," he said as he turned away, "including the tea. Just give me a call for refills."

"I swear," Celia muttered, "that man grows more familiar every day."

"Maybe," Jen agreed dryly. "But, keep in mind, he is one of the best chefs in the city."

Her mother surprised Jen by smiling at her. "Well," she conceded, "there is that," she added, continuing to peck daintily at her meal.

The rest of the women, including Jen, set to devouring every morsel on their plates. Before they had reached the fruit salad, her mother patted her lips with her linen napkin and set back her chair.

"I have a bridge date this afternoon, Jennifer." She sent a friendly smile around the table. "Enjoy the rest of your time together, girls. It was nice seeing you all again." She hesitated in the doorway. "We'll be leaving for the Terrells' at nine o'clock, Jennifer."

"I'll be ready," Jen replied.

With the stature of a queen, she walked away, a chorus of goodbyes following her.

"The Terrells'?" Marcie said the minute the door closed behind Celia. "Are you actually going to that old people's party?"

"I am," Jen said on a sigh. "But this is the last year. It really isn't just old people who go. There are still some younger ones there."

"And every one of the young lions hell-bent on kissing butt to get to the top." Kathie's voice held an acid tint.

"That's the name of the game, isn't it?" Leslie observed. "Wasn't that the reason we all decided to get our degrees and concentrate on breaking through the glass ceiling?"

Marcie grinned. "I opted out by grabbing my delicious husband and immediately having his babies."

Jen felt a funny pang in her chest at her friend's innocent mention of marriage and babies.

"Speaking of delicious, Jennifer, it's time you told us what in the hell is going on with you and Marsh Grainger," Leslie said.

"Yes," said Mary. "Let's get down to discussing something way more interesting than a fusty old party or our careers."

Jen took a deep breath, and launched into her story. She decided not to tell her friends exactly what had sent her fleeing from her parents' house—she did truly believe that what her parents did was their own business. All she said was that there had been an issue, and she'd decided it was time to strike out on her own and get some distance.

And that was how she ended up working for—and living with—Marshall Grainger.

Her friends were all ears—until they were all questions. This time, their questions were serious.

Jen launched into a recitation of her activities since accepting Marsh's offer of employment. She told them everything having to do with the job. But for reasons she couldn't quite explain, she left out the personal side of the story.

They wanted to know what he was like to work for, and whether he was as tough and aloof as gossip described him.

And they also wanted to know how she kept from jumping his bones.

"I've got strong principles, and he has a bad rep," she

said, and they believed her. It was the truth, to some degree. Jen stood by her principles, and Marsh did have a reputation for using women...but, she had fallen for him. And, after all, he had asked her to marry him.

But for reasons she couldn't entirely explain, she didn't tell her friends about that. She could tell by the expressions on their faces that they weren't buying her story, but they knew when to quit, and didn't press her. When her story came to an end, too much time had passed and her friends needed to go. With hugs and promises to stay in touch, they went their separate ways.

Jen went back to the patio to begin clearing the table. Tony was beside her as she reached for a second plate.

"I'll take care of that," he said, moving her out of the way with a nudge. "You ladies sounded like you were having a good time."

Jen's smile was soft. "Yes, we did have a lovely time. Your lunch was superb."

He flashed a bright smile at her. "Thank you, ma'am, that's what I like to hear." His eyes teased her. "Now go away and let me do my job."

"Yes, sir, master chef," Jen said. "But never say I didn't offer to help."

He waved a hand as she walked into the dining room from the patio.

Back in her room, Jen glanced at the bedside clock. It was a little after three and her mother had said they'd be leaving at nine. Six hours. Time enough to do the ranch books before she needed to get ready.

Clicking on to her laptop, Jen logged in to the ranch accounts and got to work untangling the facts and figures the technology-challenged foreman tossed into the PC at the ranch. It didn't take her long to straighten out the mess, pay the couple of bills due and cut the checks for the employees.

After logging off the ranch server, she decided she might as well wrap up the end-of-week with the home books.

Home. The word filled her mind and brought a wave of longing so intense Jen gave a soft gasp. Marsh.

Oh, Lord, she wanted to go home. To Marsh.

Damn. Damn, damn. What in the world was she going to do? He had proposed to her. But he didn't want *her,* the person. He wanted her body, and she readily admitted, at least to herself if not to her friends, that she wanted him as badly.

But he didn't really want *her*.

He wanted an assistant, a cook, a housekeeper, a wife, a mother to his children. And she, Jennifer Dunning, would do. It didn't hurt that she was bright as well as beautiful.

Big flipping deal.

Feeling her eyes begin to sting with threatening tears, Jen closed the computer, set it aside and curled into a ball on her bed. Impatiently, she brushed her fingers over her eyes. She wouldn't cry. Not over the high and mighty Marshall Grainger. She damn well would not cry.

Jen sobbed into her pillow.

She woke to darkness. Reaching out her arm, she flicked on the lamp on the bedside table and stared bleary-eyed at the clock set next to it. It read 7:10 p.m.

Time to get it together, she told herself, dragging her listless body from the bed.

Her face was a mess. Shoulders slumped, Jen stared at the sorry excuse for a woman reflected back at her from the wide bathroom mirror above the sink. Salty tracks of dried tears lay stiff on her cheeks.

Pathetic.

With an impatient shake of her head, Jen set to work on making herself presentable. It wasn't easy. She still felt tired. That in itself was annoying as she rarely felt tired, especially not emotionally tired. The last thing she wanted was to put on that stupid costume and pile makeup on her face. Heaving a sigh, she adjusted the water temperature and stepped into the shower.

Fifteen minutes later, her body glowing from the hot shower and her hair hanging in dripping tendrils down her back, she stood shivering as she wrapped herself into a long fluffy bath sheet.

As soon as her body was dry, she went to work on her hair. Drying her hair was always a project—there was so much of it, a veritable mass of blond locks that became tumbled waves and curls as it dried. But, at last, she turned off the appliance and pulled on her lacy panties before facing the next challenge.

Standing before the dresser mirror, Jen set about piling her hair on top of her head, fastening it there so she could slip on a net cap. The cap would contain her hair beneath the wig of long, riotous black curls she had bought on impulse.

After more than a few *damns* and some stronger words, Jen had the wig securely fastened in place.

Deciding it didn't look half-bad, she shook her head. The wig stayed in place and long black curls went flying wildly around her head and down over her shoulders.

Offering her image a smile of satisfaction, she went to work on the makeup. Being a blonde, Jen was naturally fair. Opening a container of makeup a shade darker than her usual shade, she applied it smoothly. Blush next, high on her cheekbones. She darkened her eyebrows with a black brow powder, and swept black mascara on her lashes. She finished with a generous coating of scarlet lipstick.

"Jenny, I hardly know you!" she said to the stranger in the mirror. She shook her head. "No, not Jenny, not even Jen." She needed a sexy, sultry name to go with this getup. She mulled it over as she stepped into the costume. Carmen? Nah, too obvious. Rosa? Nope. "Margarita." She drew the name out in a throaty voice. Yeah! Perfect. Now, a big spray of perfume, a pair of black soft leather ballet flats and—

Stepping back, she perused her reflection. Damn if she didn't look terrific—and nearly unrecognizable. She inched the top of the full-sleeved blouse to the edge of her left shoulder, leaving it there. On the right, she nudged the thin material off the shoulder. Tucking the blouse into the skirt, she wrapped a chain belt around her waist, attaching an empty jewelry pouch into which she then slipped her cell phone, a key to her parents' house and some money. She gave the skirt a shake. The folds swirled around her ankles.

Jen topped the outfit off with large gold hoop earrings, a four-strand gold jangle necklace and a shawl in blending shades of black, sand, dark green and a splash of magenta.

Lifting her arms she swept the shawl in an arc and settled it over her shoulders.

Now she was ready.

Her parents were waiting for her in the foyer. "Oh, I'm sorry, am I late?" She hadn't bothered to look at the clock.

"Not at all, we just came down," her father answered.

"And may I say you look fantastic, Jennifer." He always called her by her full name.

"Yes, you do," her mother agreed. "Very effective."

Jen gave them a brilliant smile, giving silent thanks for the candid explanation her mother had offered her concerning the situation with the Terrells. "Thank you," she replied, shifting a glance from one to the other. "And you two look absolutely fantastic."

Her father opened the door to usher them out. "The car's right out front. Off we go to the Halloween gala."

For the last time, Jen thought to herself. She was never going to the Terrells' party again. It was time to make some changes in her life. She was going to figure out what she wanted to do about Marsh, about her living situation, about everything.

After tonight, her life was going to be totally different. One way or another.

Ten

The dance, the last of more than she could recall, finally ended. Her breathing a bit heavy from the fast-paced number, Jen smiled at her surprisingly spry elderly partner as he thanked her before walking away.

It was hot in the room. The place was jammed. Jen was sweaty and tired of the party. She was tired of dancing, too. It was time to get out of there.

Lifting a corner of the shawl she had tied around her waist, she dabbed at perspiration dampening her neck. She was smoothing the shawl back into place when she felt a long-fingered hand curve around her waist.

"You've danced with just about every man here tonight."

His voice was a rough whisper close to her ear. "I think this one is mine."

A chill chased the heat from her neck all the way down to the base of her spine.

Marsh.

"Not talking to me?" He nipped gently at her ear.

Jen had to swallow. He was pressed against her back. Talk to him? She could barely breathe. "Why…why didn't you tell me you were going to be here?"

"It was a last-minute decision." His arm moved, turning her to face him.

He looked dangerous, and delicious. He had dressed as a gentleman of years past, out for a night at the opera or theater. He was wearing what she'd wager was his own hand-tailored tuxedo, black tie and pleated, blazing white shirt. He also had on a silk top hat, a long black cape with a stand-up collar, and held a silver-handled black walking stick.

Breathtaking.

He started moving against her sensuously, suggestively, enticing her to dance with him. She raised her gaze to his. His eyes glimmered with intent like sunstruck silver.

"I watched you dancing." He lowered his head to murmur against her ear. "You dance very well. Will you dance with me?"

Dance? She could barely move. His hard body pressed against hers was sapping all the strength from her. She felt light-headed. She had to get out before she made a fool of herself by collapsing at his feet.

"No, I don't want to dance." Jen hardly recognized her own voice it was so dry and shaky. "I want to get some air."

Marsh moved back a bit to look into her face. The smile he gave her was positively wicked. "With me?"

"I just want to leave, please."

"I can't resist a lady who says please."

Keeping his arm around her waist, Marsh turned and

headed for the front entrance, sweeping her along with him as he strode toward the door.

"Wait." Jen halted abruptly as she came to her senses. "I must tell my parents I'm leaving." She turned out of his embrace only to feel his arms slide around her waist as he turned with her.

"I'll come with you," he said.

"Marsh," she began.

He set his brows into an arrogant arch. "You're ashamed to be seen with me?"

"No, no." Jen shook her head. She wasn't ashamed, just terrified of what he might say to her parents. "I just, well, I believe they are having a conversation with friends."

He didn't bother to respond as he piloted her toward the pair standing near the long buffet table.

Jen braced herself as he came to a stop before her parents. "Mother," she managed, pausing to wet her lips. "I'm leaving now."

"I see," her mother responded, a suspicious gleam in her eyes. "Aren't you going to introduce your friend?"

"No need," her father said, a friendly smile on his face. He extended his hand. "Marsh, I'd like you to meet my wife, Celia."

"A pleasure," Marsh said.

Celia arched a brow. "Are you escorting Jennifer, Mr. Grainger?"

"Yes, ma'am," he responded in a tone of respect.

"Mmm," she murmured again, eyeing Marsh up and down.

Jen's stomach clenched in apprehension.

Her father laughed. "Celia, I think you need a glass of champagne. Run along, Jennifer." He turned a stern look on Marsh. "You will take care of her." It was not even close to a question.

"Yes, sir," Marsh answered at once.

Nodding, her father murmured good-night and, taking Celia's hand, led her away.

Marsh was chuckling as he took a stunned Jen to the door. "Do you have your car?"

They were outside. Jen drew a deep breath. The air had turned cold. It hit her flushed skin like an Arctic blast chilling her exposed flesh. Loosening the filmy shawl from around her waist she drew it around her shoulders. "No, I came with my parents."

"Good." Taking her hand, he led her to his car, a sleek black Lincoln parked right in front of the large house.

"You left your car here?" Jen said, sliding into the passenger seat when he opened the door for her.

He slid behind the wheel and slanted a look at her. "I wasn't planning on staying."

"Then why bother to come at all?"

"I came to collect you…and you know it."

The grin he flashed created a shudder in her lower regions. Now, even with the chill air, Jen felt hotter than she had in the house, and it had nothing to do with the thin shawl.

"Where are we going?" she said, turning to look out the window. "My parents live in the other direction."

"I know where your parents live, Jen," he said. "We're going to my place here in town. We'll be there in a few minutes."

"I didn't know you had a place in town." The thought that she and Marsh would be alone soon, at his place, a place that presumably had a bedroom, was almost more than Jen could bear. She simultaneously wanted to flee from him and tell him to drive faster.

Jen glanced out the window. They were in the heart of the city, tall office buildings looming over the car. Marsh turned onto a ramp leading to the private underground parking lot of one of the tallest buildings. Inserting a card into a pad on the chain-link gate, the gate silently slid open, and silently closed again after he drove through.

She knew at once where they were. This parking lot, the building towering overhead, contained the corporate headquarters of his business. *Grainger Building* in bold brass letters arched over the double front doors at the main entrance. She had passed it many times.

"You live here?" she asked as he pulled the car into a spot marked Private.

"No." Marsh shook his head as he swung open his door. "I keep this place for when I have to be in town for business reasons."

Although he circled the car, Jen was out before he got to her. "Convenient."

"Come along," he said, lifting the cape to swirl it around her shoulders. "You're shivering."

Warmth from his body intensifying the shiver, Jen moved with him to the door. He inserted another computerized key card into a barely noticeable slot. Shiny brass elevator doors parted with a soft swish.

Inside he pushed an unmarked button. The door swished shut and the car began to rise…quickly.

The penthouse, Jen thought. The car came to a smooth stop and the doors again softly swished apart.

Marsh's arm still firmly around her waist, he took her with him when he stepped from the car.

To Jen's surprise they didn't step directly into the

penthouse but into a spacious lobby. Still moving her with him, he crossed the lobby to the only door visible. He drew out another card to open the door.

Pushing the door open, Marsh swept out his arm, inviting her inside.

"Step into my parlor," Jen murmured, catching her breath as she entered. What she could see of the place was absolutely elegant.

"You consider yourself the fly?" Marsh said in reference to her quote, amusement woven through his voice.

"And you the spider," Jen said, shrugging out from beneath his cloak and handing it to him.

"Is that the way you think of me?" Although his voice was even, she caught the slight edge to it.

Jen turned to meet his steely gaze.

"No, not at all," she answered without hesitation. "I was being a smart-mouth."

Some of the glitter faded from his eyes. "Are you afraid of me, Jen?"

"Of course not." She protested the very idea. "Why should…" She paused, holding his steady gaze, changing her tune. "Do I have reason to be afraid, Marsh?"

Smiling, he shook his head. "No, Jennifer, you don't. If you'll recall, I asked you to marry me."

She glanced away. "I do remember."

"I'm still waiting for an answer."

Jen moved into the room, over to the floor-to-ceiling windows. The view of the city lights from the top of the building gave her an altogether different perception of it than from the street.

"It's beautiful," she murmured, speaking more to herself than to him.

"Yes." He came up behind her, sliding one arm around her waist. "And I'm still waiting for an answer."

She closed her eyes. "Marsh, I just don't know. I...I..."

"Don't," he murmured. This time his lips brushed her ear, bringing a flutter to her chest and heat flooding to parts south. "I can wait for your answer, at least to that question. But I need to know if you'll stay with me here tonight, Jennifer." His voice was warm, rich, deep—she could feel it vibrating through her down to her toes.

"Yes, Marsh," she answered against her will. "I will stay with you tonight."

Applying light pressure to her waist, he drew her closer. "Now, for the price of one kiss—a scorcher, mind you—I'll give you the guided tour of the apartment. Deal?" He grinned.

"Deal," she echoed, leaning into him and bringing her hands up to cradle his face, drawing him to her.

His mouth gently touched hers. But Jen was having none of it. He had said a scorcher, and that was what he was going to get.

She nipped at his bottom lip before taking his mouth with her own in a silent demand. Marsh was quick to comply, taking over the kiss with the expertise of experienced mastery.

A low groan deep in her throat, Jen melted into him, returning his kiss with all the passion she'd been unable to express since she'd left Marsh a day ago. His tongue invaded. She met the attack with a thrust of her own. It was wonderful, exciting, nearly overwhelming.

But it was not enough. She wanted more, much more, and from the sensation of him pressing against her belly, she had no doubt he felt the same.

Finally, needing more air, she eased back a few inches to gaze into his eyes.

"Can we put off the grand tour until tomorrow?"

she asked between quickly drawn breaths. "I need to be naked and in bed with you."

"Now you're talking." Sweeping her up into his arms, Marsh strode from the living room into his bedroom. It was dimly lit by the lights in buildings outside. All Jen noticed was that the room was large...and his bed took up the majority of space.

She began working on the buttons of his shirt. He already had her blouse on the floor. Within moments their clothing lay scattered around the bed, decorating the carpet. Marsh had his teeth clamped on the corner of a silver package he had removed from his trouser pocket before dropping his pants to the floor. She could see he wanted to be inside her as much as she wanted him there.

Tossing back the bedcovers, and once again lifting her, he settled her in the center of the bed and stretched his long length beside her. His skin felt like warm silk over long tight muscles.

Jen already felt hot and desperate with need for him. The feel of him moving over her, on top of her, shattered the last of her swiftly fading inhibitions. Moaning, she moved restlessly against him, parting her legs in invitation.

His reaction was swift. Grasping her hips, he dragged her into full contact with his steel-hard erection.

She shuddered in anticipation.

Jen braced her hands on his chest but suddenly he was gone. She murmured a protest but swallowed it when she opened her eyes to see him applying the condom.

"Let's be smart this time," he said.

Jen was surprised but too desperate to have him inside

her to say anything. Lifting her hips again, he moved into her, sheathing himself deeply within her heat.

"Yes," she whispered, closing her eyes again. Then, "Oh, yes," as he began to rotate his hips, delving deeper, deeper into her body.

Jen had never believed the stories told by women about crying out when reaching climax. She became a believer moments later, calling his name in a hoarse voice she barely recognized as her own as her body appeared to shatter into a million pieces.

Marsh's cry echoed her own. Head thrown back, tendons straining in his neck, he stiffened an instant before wrapping his arms around her. Jen was drawing shaky breaths into her depleted body when Marsh, still buried deep inside her, gently lowered his tension-taut body against hers, his indrawn breath as raw as her own.

"Marsh?" Jen forced out his name between gulps for oxygen. "Are you all right?"

"Yeah," he answered, his warm breath tickling her ear. "But for a moment there, I felt certain I had died."

"Yeah," she echoed. "Me, too."

"Wanna try it again?"

Jen expelled a breath in a burst of laughter. "Are you kidding? I can barely breathe." She hesitated a mere instant before adding, "Give me a second."

"Okay," he said, nipping at the soft skin beneath her chin.

Jen slid from under him and made her way to the bathroom. Finding a light switch, she flipped it, stifling a gasp of appreciation at the opulence of the room. There was a lot of marble, swirls of dark chocolate and white, and a huge tub with all kinds of gadgets she was tempted to play with. A long wooden-slatted bench sat next to a walk-in shower stall along one wall. On the facing wall, an even longer vanity cabinet with two sinks and an array of interesting-looking bottles and jars and candles was set below a mirror in exact proportion to the cabinet.

For a moment, Jen was sorely tempted to jump into the shower stall for a quick sluice over her sweaty skin. But she decided she'd much rather get back to Marsh as fast as she could.

Her eyes widened as she came back to the bed and saw one of the most beautiful sights she'd ever seen in her life. Marsh, buck naked and rock hard…again.

She took advantage of the moment to admire his fantastic body as he opened another package and put the condom on.

Ready for him, Jen curled her arms around his neck, sighing with contentment as he settled himself in the cradle between her thighs.

"How could you have…" She didn't know how to finish asking how he had revived so quickly.

Marsh just smiled at her and said, "Maybe it has something to do with the fact that you are the sexiest thing I've ever seen, Jen."

Jen would have thought that the second time the pace would be slower, easier. And it might have been, if she had allowed Marsh to set the pace. But Jen shocked herself with her need, her hunger, touching him, tasting him everywhere. Within moments he was inside her again, taking, giving, demanding, pleading. It was too fast, too intense, too hot and over much too soon.

Marsh barely grunted before collapsing on top of her, harsh breaths bathing the curve of her neck, sending delicious shivers up her spine. And though his voice was little more than a whisper, she heard what he said.

"Jennifer, Jennifer…you are one amazing woman."

"I know," she said in the best demure tone she could manage, a satisfied smile curving her well-kissed mouth.

Lifting his body onto his forearms, Marsh threw back his head and roared with laughter. He was still laughing when his mouth came crashing down again on hers, his tongue diving deep, claiming her as his own.

"I adore you," he said, when he was forced to break away to breathe. "Marry me."

Jen ached at his words. She wanted to confess that she couldn't marry him, because he *adored* her but didn't love her. But something stopped her from telling Marsh the truth—she simply couldn't do it. "I told you, Marsh. I must have more time to think about it."

He heaved a heavy sigh of frustration. "Dammit, Jen, what's to think about? We're compatible. We work well together. More importantly, we have fun together. And you wouldn't dare tell me we're not great together in bed." A tiny shudder rippled through him. "I swear to you that never before in my life have I experienced anything even close to what I've just shared with you."

Jen opened her mouth to respond, to say it was more about sex than any deep, meaningful affection but he wasn't finished.

"And damned if I'm not getting hard again."

This time Jen bypassed demure and went straight for wanton. "So please shut up and do the same thing to me again."

Marsh did…again and again throughout the rest of the night and into the early morning hours.

Jen opened her eyes to bright sunlight pouring through the wall of windows onto her face. Groaning a protest, she immediately shut them again.

"Hit the white button on the nightstand." Marsh's breath fluttered the hair at her temple.

Squinting, Jen reached out, her hand groping for the button. Her fingers barely brushed it. With a soft swish filmy curtains slid from the ends of the windows to join together in the center, defusing the brightness of the midday sunlight.

"Oh, lovely," Jen murmured, daring to open her eyes again. She turned her head to find Marsh's silver eyes watching her. She smiled. "Good morning."

"Morning." He smiled back at her. "God, you're beautiful."

"I'm sure." Jen laughed as an image of what she must look like in the light of day after the night they had spent practically devouring each other. She dreaded looking at what all that activity had done to her gypsy-girl makeup.

"Oh, you are, Jen. You look all tousled and heavy-lidded, like a woman well loved."

Well screwed, Jen thought, a bitter taste at the back of her throat. He didn't mean *loved.* Not the way she wanted him to mean it. In that instant, she wanted to go. She had to go. She felt queasy. Tossing back the covers, she slipped from the bed and dashed into the bathroom, locking the door behind her. She could barely hear Marsh calling to her.

"Hey, Jen, what the hell?"

After cleaning the makeup from her face the best she could, Jen stood in the shower, her tears mingling with the drumming water splashing over her head. *He doesn't believe in love. He doesn't believe in love.* The phrase repeated inside her head, keeping time with the spill of shower water. She cried harder than she imagined possible, trying to be silent so Marsh wouldn't hear. She felt as if her heart were breaking in two.

Later, standing dripping on the shower mat, Jen didn't remember bathing or shampooing her hair, yet her body was wet, her hair soaked. Picking up one of the bath sheets folded and piled on the slatted bench, she slowly dried her body, trying not to think about all the amazing things Marsh had done to her the night before.

Her hair was still dripping water down her back. There were two round stiff-bristled men's hair brushes set to one side of the vanity top. Picking up the nearest to her, she worked at brushing the tangles from her mass of thick hair, perhaps harder than she needed to. When she finished, the hair lay smooth against her shoulders and the brush was matted with her blond hair. She looked closer and saw that her hair was tangled in the brush with his.

She left it there.

Jen was about to wrap her shivering body in the wet towel she had discarded when she turned and noticed a dark brown terry robe hanging from a hook on the door. Dropping the towel into a large open basket, she shrugged into the robe. It was the softest, warmest robe she had ever touched. Clutching the robe close, she drew a deep, courage-gathering breath and, opening the door, strode back into the lion's den.

The particular lion waiting there for her looked relaxed stretched out in all his naked glory on the bed, his long, lean body bathed in sunlight. But the relaxed look was deceiving. The glitter in his narrowed silver eyes gave him away.

"Jennifer, what's going on?" His voice was low, but edged with concern.

"Nothing." Unable to bear looking at the sheer mas-

culine beauty of him, Jen turned away, grimacing at
the sight of her discarded clothing littering the floor,
the costume seeming so silly and forced in the morning light.

"Nothing, huh?" The concern in his voice hardened.
"Then what the hell are you doing?"

Scooping up her panties and the now crumpled skirt
she had worn, Jen slowly turned to look at him. Although she hadn't heard him move, Marsh was now
sitting on the side of the bed, the sheet pulled up to
his waist.

Jen swallowed to moisten her parched throat. "I'm
picking up my clothes to get dressed."

"Why?" His tone was flat, his expression passive.

"Why?" She shook her head as if in disbelief he
had asked the question. "It's after noon. It's time I get
home." A pure bald-faced lie if Jen had ever told one,
especially given the fact that the only place she now
considered home was next to Marsh. She fought as hard
as she could not to cry.

"Are you concerned about getting home, or do you
have a case of morning-after remorse?"

"No remorse," she said as calmly as she could, thinking that she would never regret a moment of the time
she had spent with Marsh. Not a moment. Straightening her spine she met his silvery gaze with a hard stare
of her own.

"No?" He arched a brow. "Then why have you
dumped me into the deep freeze?"

"You keep at me," she said, scrambling for a way to
protect herself against him, a way to keep herself from
telling him the truth. "I told you I need more time." She
paused, seeing something new in Marsh's eyes for a
moment, something she couldn't quite identify yet. She

relented a little—she couldn't help herself. "I haven't dumped you into the deep freeze."

He arched a brow at her. "Feels damn chilly to me."

"I'm sorry." That was the truth, she suddenly realized. She *was* sorry. Why blame him for the fact that she foolishly fell in love with him? It wasn't his fault her heart was choosing him even though her head was saying no. "I just don't like being pressured."

"Okay, I'll back off…for a while." His piercing gaze softened as a small smile crept across his mouth.

Oh, heavens, his mouth. Jen could feel his talented mouth, could taste him. He looked good enough to eat. The thought abruptly brought her to her senses, reminding her that she needed to get out, to get away from Marsh before she fell back into bed with him, and then found herself crying in the bathroom again, her heart breaking into pieces.

"Thank you." Bending again, she scooped the now crushed blouse from the floor. "But I still want to go home." As she retrieved the black wig, she wrinkled her nose with distaste at the thought of putting the costume back on in order to go home. What had she been thinking last night?

She hadn't been thinking at all, clearly.

"You don't have to wear those clothes to go, even though you did look sexy as hell in your costume. Turned me on something awful," he said, rising to stroll to the bathroom. "We'll find you something to wear."

In an effort to conceal a shiver of response to his admitted sensual reaction to her gypsy attire, Jen held the robe's two sides together, snuggling into the soft terry warmth. "Thanks."

"I'm going to grab a shower, then I'll drive you home." The bathroom door closed quietly behind him.

Recalling the night they had spent together in his king-size bed, her wanton surrender to him, Jen sank, weak-kneed, into a deeply cushioned chair. Biting her lip, her bravado show of spirit deflated, she glanced around for her small string bag. It lay on the floor, next to the chair she had sunk into.

A sigh whispered through her slightly parted lips.

She loved him, more with each passing day. The time she'd spent without him had seemed interminable from the time she'd left the house until he had slipped his arm around her at the party. She longed to be with him every day, sleep beside him every night…

Jen heard the shower running full force. Her imagination instantly produced an image of Marsh, the water falling over his perfectly formed, magnificent body. Heat rushed to the most sensitive part of her body.

Closing her eyes, she leaned back against the chair. His sexy, masculine scent clung to his robe, increasing the heat now radiating throughout her body.

She wanted to be with him, ached for him so badly she had to resist a compulsion to shrug out of the robe and join him in the shower, join with him under the pounding spray.

No. Think, she railed at herself. *Back away. Now.*

While you still have a modicum of resistance in your mind, if not your body.

The sound of the rushing water ceased. Jen went stiff. In the moments it took him to towel off and walk back into the bedroom, she had made her decision and closed her eyes, as if closing him out of her life as well as her view.

She could not go on this way, loving him heart and soul, knowing all the while he did not love her. Eventually, it would kill something inside of her, something that made up who she was.

"Ready?"

Jen opened her eyes. Marsh was smiling at her. His smile went through her like a knife. Dragging up an ounce of fortitude from deep inside, she managed to return his smile without breaking down.

"Yes." The mere whisper was all she could manage.

They left the penthouse together after Marsh found her a shirt and a pair of shorts that practically came down to her knees. Fortunately, he didn't touch her as they walked to his car. Had he so much as touched her elbow, she was afraid she'd fall apart.

They rode in silence to her parents' home some miles out of the city. The ride seemed to take forever. Jen already had her door key in hand when Marsh steered the car up the driveway and to a smooth stop next to the broad sweep of steps to the porch.

She was ready with her hand on the door release, prepared to bolt and run. But Marsh touched her arm. It was a light touch that felt to Jen as though it scorched her arm to the bone.

"I'm going straight back to the house from here," he said, a slight frown drawing his eyebrows together. "Are you driving back today or waiting until tomorrow morning?"

Jen wet her lips. She had to tell him she wouldn't be going back to his house, that she couldn't bear being with him, loving him and knowing he didn't love her. She should have told him before they left the condo, but she simply couldn't, not then. And she didn't think she could now, either.

"Probably tomorrow morning," she said, lying through her teeth. "Less traffic then."

His silvery gaze probed hers for a moment. Then he removed his hand from her arm. "Okay."

"Goodbye, Marsh." The words hurt like fire in her mouth. She pushed the door open, slammed it shut and took off running, unable to look back for fear that she'd go straight back to him and tell him that yes, she would spend the rest of her life with him.

Even if he didn't love her.

Eleven

Where the hell is she?

Marsh frowned at the recurring question stabbing at his mind, unconscious of his fingertips smoothing the silky material of the shawl Jennifer had left in his car when he had dropped her off on Sunday afternoon.

Or more accurately, when she had practically run away from him after he had dropped her off Sunday afternoon.

There was something going on with her, something she wasn't telling him. But the more pressing issue at the moment was, where the hell was she?

If she had left her parents' home Monday morning, or even later in the day, she would have been back at the house before dark. It was now Wednesday evening, and there had been no sight or sound of Jen.

If something had happened to her—an accident, or illness—Marsh was certain he would have heard about it by now. He had called her cell phone only to receive a request to leave a message. Cursing, he had disconnected. He didn't want to talk to voice mail, he wanted to talk to Jen. Swallowing his pride, he had called her parents' phone, only to be informed by the housekeeper that the family was not at home.

Marsh got that message loud and clear. The family, including Jen, would not be accepting calls from him. So, no, there had been no accident, nor was she ill. And she didn't wish to speak to him.

Maybe it was time to face the fact that Jen was not coming back.

You damn dumb ass, Marsh condemned himself. He had pushed her too hard in his bid to convince her to marry him. And now he ached for her like he had never ached for anyone, ever—not just for the nearly unbelievable pleasure he had achieved with her, but for simply being with her, being near her, conversing, laughing, even arguing.

He began to pace the length of his large office, memories swirling of their time together.

Jen humming as she went about her work.

Jen laughing as they raced the horses.

Jen deftly cooking up a meal fit for a king…for him.

Coming to a dead stop, Marsh closed his eyes. Because he had wrapped himself in bitterness and convinced himself he didn't believe in love, he had carelessly thrown away the most precious gift ever offered to him.

Suddenly, as if he had been smacked upside his head, Marsh leapt from his chair.

He was in love with her.

He was *in love* with her.

What was wrong with him? How could it have taken him so damn long to come to that conclusion?

He had to talk to her, tell her, beg if necessary. She had to know how he felt. That would change everything.

Wouldn't it?

But what if she hadn't come back because she didn't—or couldn't—love him?

He suddenly remembered why he didn't believe in love. Or rather, why he didn't actually want anything to do with love. Because it made people crazy. It made them do weird things. And people who claimed to love other people didn't necessarily treat them the way they should be treated. He knew about that firsthand.

Get over it, he told himself. This was his chance. Jen was his opportunity. She was the one. If he blew this, then it wouldn't matter one way or the other whether he believed in loved because he would never get a chance to try ever again.

He had to tell her. And he had do it as soon as possible.

A soft tearing sound caught Marsh's attention. Frowning, he glanced down at his hand, his long fingers tangled in her shawl. He had ripped the fine fabric.

Cursing himself, Marsh set the shawl aside before he could do more damage to it. There was an elderly woman in San Antonio he knew who was sheer magic with a needle. She would mend it so perfectly, Jen would never see the tear.

Glad for something positive to do—as he sure as hell hadn't accomplished much by mentally beating himself up for being an unconscious moron—Marsh picked up his phone and dialed the woman's number.

Minutes later, Marsh roared through the gates of the

property heading for San Antonio, the carefully folded shawl on the seat next to him.

He was going to fix it. He was going to fix everything.

Jen drove through the gates to Marsh's house. As always, she hit the horn and waved to greet the security guard parked in the all-wheel vehicle nearly hidden beneath the lone tree at the top of the knoll.

Jen was nervous. Although throughout the past couple of days she had repeatedly vowed to herself, and aloud to her empty room, that she would not return to Marsh, here she was, feeling much too at home for her mental comfort.

Pulling to a stop at the garage, Jen knew at once Marsh wasn't home because his truck was gone.

What if he had driven to Dallas to coax her back to the house—and to him?

Jen stopped dead in her tracks, caught between a burst of laughter and a cry of despair. As if the confident and arrogant Marshall Grainger would ever conceive of crawling, or even boldly striding, to any woman to beg her to return to him.

The mere thought was ludicrous. At any rate, it didn't matter. She had no intention of remaining at the house. She had returned only to turn down Marsh's offer, then immediately head back to Dallas as soon as she had collected her personal belongings. She had planned to tell him face-to-face, and even admit to him that the reason she couldn't marry him was because she loved him, and knew that he'd never love her.

Maybe it was better that he wasn't there. It was definitely safer for her. In truth, she ached to see him, but she feared what she would do if she did. Whatever it was, it would probably lead to her being in a loveless marriage, and that would tear her apart inside. No, it was better this way.

Heaving a sigh, Jen went straight to the apartment. As the temperature had again climbed into the sixties after dropping into the low fifties for two days, the apartment smelled stale and felt stuffy.

Crossing to a living room window, she flipped back the lock and opened it just as Marsh's truck growled to a stop next to her once-again-dusty Cadillac.

A thrill went through her as she saw his long legs stretch out from the cab and reach to the ground. A frown creased his brow as he stared at her car.

Jen stepped back from the window as he turned to glance up before striding to the garage entrance. Knowing he was headed for her apartment, she stood, quivering inside, gathering her composure to project a show of confidence.

He knocked on the door. Jen was stunned for a moment. Fully expecting him to walk in as if he owned the place—which in fact he did—she stared at the door, her mind frozen.

"Jennifer?"

For a second, she had a crazy urge to hide so that if he did walk in, he wouldn't see her. And she wouldn't have to tell him what she came to say. But she'd put it off too long. It was time to come clean. That promise she'd made herself before the gala about her life being different one way or the other? Now was the time to make that a reality.

"I'm coming," she answered, wetting her dry lips as she crossed to the door. She swung it wide as she stepped back.

A jumble of all sorts of emotions welled up inside

her at the sight of him. Dressed in a soft chambray shirt tucked into the slim waistband of his well-worn jeans that covered the tops of his scuffed boots, his hair tousled as if from his fingers raking through the silky strands, he looked…

He looked like the man she was so desperately in love with. Damn him.

"Is it Monday already?" he drawled, running a slow glance over the length of her body and back again to settle on her eyes. He took a step toward her.

Jen stepped back. "Marsh, please don't." She raised a palm to halt his progress.

As if she could.

Walking to her, he pulled her into his arms, bent his head and crushed her mouth with his.

Jen was a goner and she knew it…but she had to try, didn't she? She had to stop him long enough to state her position.

"Marsh…I can't," she began.

"Yes, you can," he murmured, barely moving his lips from hers. "And very well, too."

To prove his point, he proceeded to show her his idea of her position, which was flat on her back, him on top of her, right there in the middle of the living room floor.

Within moments boots, jeans and underwear were gone. Although she protested, her protests were weak, and so was she—weak with her need for him.

His mouth devoured hers, his hands gripping her hips—she fully expected him to ram into her. Then, something incredible happened. Instead of taking her with the passionate force she'd become accustomed to, Marsh entered her body with exquisite gentleness, slowly, as if savoring every movement until he was fully, deeply inside her, filling the emptiness she'd been denying she felt.

"Home."

His voice was so low, Jen wasn't certain she'd heard him correctly.

He began to move and within seconds she was moaning, moving with his increased thrusts, craving more and more of him, enough to last her a lifetime.

It was more intense than ever before, her release wildly shattering. Tears filling her eyes, she drew deep breaths, reminding herself of what she had to do.

They lay side by side, naked from the waist down. As her breathing returned to normal, Jen steeled herself to speak.

Marsh beat her to it. "I really didn't think it was possible to reach such intense sexual pleasure, the absolute zenith of orgasms."

The tears, stinging hot, overflowed Jen's eyes to roll down her temples into her hair. "Marsh." Her nails dug into the plush nap of the carpet. "I came here today to get my stuff…to tell you I can't stay with you, that I…"

Feeling him grow still beside her, she broke off.

"What?" His voice was soft but rough-edged. "Say it, Jennifer. Say whatever it is you have to say."

Ignoring the spill of tears on her face, she turned her head to look at him, and immediately wished she hadn't.

His silvery eyes glittering, he held her misty gaze. Were there tears in his eyes? She couldn't tell, because he got to his feet fast, in one fluid movement. Scooping his clothes and boots from the floor, he turned and strode to the door.

"I'm going to clean up," he said, his voice tight. "We'll talk about this when I get back." Not bothering to wait for a reply, he walked out, leaving the door wide-open behind him.

Rising, Jen was not nearly as fluid as Marsh had been.

She was still shaking with the aftershocks of the intensity of pleasure rippling through her body, and the pain in her heart.

She had come here determined to break off the untenable relationship she had been sharing with Marsh. Instead, she had betrayed herself by surrendering at his first kiss.

Gathering her clothing and boots while trying to pull her composure together, Jen headed for the bathroom. Positive Marsh would not be gone for long, she pulled her clothes back on and tried to get herself together.

Jen was brushing her hair when Marsh strolled back into the apartment and without hesitation opened the bathroom door and stood there, simply watching her.

Jen considered a protest then rejected the idea…it would simply be a waste of her breath. Setting aside the brush, she walked past him into the living room. Turning, she stood tall, placed her hands on her hips and stared back at him in open defiance.

"So. You're going to run, from me and what we've got together?" His voice roughened. "What we've just shared together?"

"Sex," Jen retorted, wincing inside at his accusation that she was going to run. Again. But this was different, she insisted in silent despair. This was for the rest of her life, not just to escape an uncomfortable situation. She wanted to stay so much, too much, but…

The sound of his voice scattered her jumbled thoughts.

"Fantastic sex," he corrected her, his voice beginning to sound strained. "But we've got more than that and you know it."

Jen was shaking her head before he'd finished. "It's not enough, Marsh."

"What the hell more do you want?" he said. "We enjoy the same things. We enjoy each other. You said you love it here at the house. What else is there?"

Jen sighed and drew a quick breath before calmly answering. "Love."

She watched Marsh take in what she'd said, and she saw something cross his face. For a moment, she allowed herself to hope, but his words made it clear that she was foolish to do so.

"We could make it work," he said, his tone strange, unfamiliar. "It's been done before, a marriage without love."

Jen's spine stiffened. So she was right. He didn't love her. He didn't love her at all.

"I don't believe I could do it," she said, forcing herself to continue on. "When I marry, I want to spend my days and nights working and sleeping beside a man I'm in love with, knowing he loves me, too."

She waited, hoping against hope that she'd been wrong, that he would tell her that he loved her more than she could know. But that's not what he said.

"I see." Shaking his head, his expression blank, he turned and walked to the door, pausing to glance back at her. "If you change your mind, you know where to find me." That said, he pulled open the door and walked out of the room.

And out of her life.

The realization was crushing. Standing rigidly still, afraid if she moved she would fall apart, Jen gasped for air, hurting so badly she wanted to drop to the floor and sob until the pain eased.

But she didn't drop to the floor, nor issue one sob. She brushed away tears with an impatient swipe of her hand.

She loved him, deeply, passionately, but she had no intentions of falling apart for him. She wasn't the type for drama—she was the type that carried on under difficult conditions.

She'd survive, Jen assured herself, beginning to gather her things together. A large shopping bag she had brought with her from home contained the shirt belonging to Marsh. Sighing, she reached into the bag to stroke the material. Tempted to take it with her, she pulled her hand back.

"You're a fool, Marshall Grainger," she muttered. "We could have built a wonderful, loving relationship and made beautiful children together."

Though soft, the sound of her own voice startled her. The word *children* rang in her mind. Once again she felt the sting of tears in her eyes. She shook her head. *It's over,* she told herself. *Get on with your life.*

The explanation Jen offered her parents for her return home was that she missed her friends and the activities in Dallas. Of course, it was far from the truth. Although Jen dearly loved her friends, they were often in touch, and Jen had never wanted to be involved with any activity in the city.

To her mother's vocal dismay, Jen was at heart a homebody. She stayed in, spending her time with Tony and Ida, cooking and keeping the house neat. A pang twisted in her chest as she recalled working in Marsh's beautiful home.

Jen spent time on her computer perusing help-wanted sites. But she wasn't looking for work. She was looking for possible postings by Marsh.

None appeared, which Jen found rather strange. Perhaps he had decided to advertise in local newspapers, she thought.

Thanksgiving came and went. Her parents went, too, setting out on a monthlong cruise. Jen threw herself into her long-held tradition of decorating the large house for Christmas with Tony and Ida. Only at weak moments did she wonder if Marsh ever bothered to decorate his house for the coming holiday.

When the house was finished, sparkling with gold and silver decorations, Jen set about shopping. She started with gifts for Tony and Ida. Then she shopped for her parents—never an easy chore as both were very particular. Yet all the while as she browsed the stores, Jen caught herself pausing to inspect an item she just knew would be perfect for Marsh.

So much for putting him out of her mind.

The most fun Jen had shopping was when she was buying gifts for her gang. They had a rule about price—no expensive gifts allowed. The idea was to find tokens of affection, not ostentatious things to impress or display.

The week before Christmas the six of them got together for lunch, and to exchange the presents. There were a lot of oohs and aahs. But as soon as the gift giving was over, and the wineglasses refilled, the interrogation began.

"What made you quit your job with Marshall Grainger?"

Jen sat quietly a moment, wondering what to say, what excuse to make up. Glancing around the table and seeing concern in each one of their faces, Jen knew only the truth would do.

"I love him," she whispered, tears welling in her eyes.

There was a collective gasp, and then her friends all reached out to her at once. The love and support she felt from them was overwhelming.

"What's the problem?" Kathie asked.

"He doesn't love me."

Everyone started to protest at once.

"Please." Jen held up a palm, blinking away the tears. "I really don't want to talk about it." Up until her blurted confession the atmosphere had been festive, happy. "This isn't the time or place."

"You never want to talk about it when you have strong feelings," Mary said.

"Which is fine," Karen insisted. "But just know that you deserve happiness, and you deserve love, and if you think Marsh is the one for you, then you have to get over your fear and tell him."

Jen was stunned into silence by her friend's speech. As a favor to her, they agreed to change the subject. But when they parted company a short time later, exchanging good wishes for the holidays and thanks for the gifts, they reminded her of what they had said.

More than a bit depressed, and feeling guilty for putting a damper on their holiday lunch, Jen drove straight home. Pulling into the driveway, she was startled to see Marsh's black Lincoln in front of the house. She could see he was in the car and felt a thrill when he turned to look at her.

She drove past him to the garage at the back of the house. She heard the purr of the Lincoln pull up next to where she'd stopped.

She got out of the car, turning to face him when he came to a halt beside her car. He was holding a plastic grocery bag in one hand and he held it aloft.

"I brought you something."

Considering the season, she naturally assumed it was a gift. "I wish you wouldn't have," she said. "I have nothing to give you—"

"It's not a Christmas gift," he said, setting her mind at ease. "It belongs to you."

"Oh."

"You might invite me inside."

Jen hesitated.

"For a few minutes?" His voice held a strange note. Was it a hint of pleading? Jen dismissed the very idea.

"All right, come in." Her key card at the ready, Jen slid it along the slot. The elevator glided open and she stepped inside the car, Marsh at her heels.

"Convenient," he said, teasing her. She couldn't help but smile at his use of the very word she'd used to describe the entrance to his apartment after the gala that night. She loved how Marsh remembered everything she said, down to the last detail.

"It goes to my late grandmother's apartment." The door slid open and Jen stepped inside, Marsh beside her.

"Yours now?" he asked, glancing around the room.

"Yes." Seeing him, being so close to him, made Jen feel teary again. The last thing she wanted was to have him see her crying. "You have something of mine?"

"Yes." He handed her the bag.

Frowning, Jen reached inside and withdrew a tissue-wrapped bundle. She unwrapped it to find the shawl she had worn to the Halloween ball. She hadn't even missed it.

"Thank you," she said, unconsciously stroking the soft material.

"You left it in my car after the gala."

Reminded of the night they had spent together, she suddenly wanted him to leave as she could feel her composure crumbling. Being around Marsh was nearly impossible.

Her friends' words rang in her ears. Should she—*could she*—tell him the truth?

He hesitated, drew a breath as if unsure of himself, then quickly said, "I do have a gift for you, if you'll accept it."

Jen didn't understand. He held nothing in his hands. "What is it?"

He took a hesitant step toward her. "It's my heart. And it's wrapped in my love for you, if you'll have it." He took another step and then another until he was mere inches from her seemingly frozen body.

Jen stared at him, unable to believe he had said what she had heard. "Marsh…"

"I know you don't love me." He swallowed as if it caused him pain. "And I know I declared years ago that I didn't believe in love." Raising his hands, he cradled her face with his palms. "I've been such an ass. I knew from the beginning that I wanted you." To her amazement, his eyes grew misty, only this time it wasn't her imagination. There were real tears there. "I just didn't realize why I wanted you so very much."

Tears now flowing from her eyes, Jen could barely speak. "Marsh, wait—"

"No." He cut her off with a shake of his head. "Let me finish. The simple truth of the answer hit me like a fist. I am so much in love with you and I don't know how to tell you. I wanted it to be romantic for you, hoping you'd begin to return my love. But I've been emotionally dead for so long, I don't know how—"

This time Jen cut him off. "Marshall Grainger, where on earth did you get the idea that I don't love you?"

He looked at her hard for a few moments. His mouth opened, but no words came out at first. "You...you do love me?"

Jen nodded, tears spilling down her cheeks. "If you don't kiss me right now, I won't be responsible for my actions."

His intense, silvery stare turned soft and warm. "What actions?" His voice was low, almost desperate with the sound of hope.

Jen smiled. "I was thinking about showing you how very much I love you. I love you, Marsh. I have for a while now."

Claiming her mouth with his, he swept her up into his arms. When they finally came up for air, he whispered, "Which way to the bedroom?"

Several hours later, Marsh stowed Jen's suitcase in his car, slid behind the wheel and started the motor. Glancing at her, he asked, "Ready to go home?"

Jen smiled. "I'm ready to go anywhere with you."

He set the car into motion, satisfied that they would soon be putting his ideas for their future into motion.

Settling into the warmed butter-soft leather seat, Jen pondered the past several hours. She still could barely believe Marsh had come to her, baring his soul while confessing his love for her.

She wanted to kick herself for all the time she had wasted being miserable away from him. All that misery could have been avoided had she just told him the truth the last time she had been to the house.

Well, the misery was now over. Marsh loved her, and Jen luxuriated in the very thought of his love.

Even so, she had remembered to take care of business, so to speak. Buzzing the kitchen phone, she had told Tony not to fuss for dinner as she would be leaving for Marsh's house within a few hours.

"I figured," the unflappable Tony replied. "I saw his car in the driveway. What about your parents?" he asked. "You remember they'll be home on the twenty-second for the holidays?"

"Yes, I remember," Jen said. "I'll be calling them with the news."

"News?" Ida, obviously listening in on one of the other extensions, asked. "There will be news?"

"Wonderful news," Jen said. "And that's all I'm saying at this time."

It was late when they arrived at Marsh's place. Stepping from the car, Jen gazed at the house, emotion tightening her throat. Home. Her glance at the tall man lifting her case from the car sent a wave of sheer contentment through her. No, she thought, as much as she loved the house, Marsh was home to her.

Not aware of him watching her, Jen started when he asked, "What are you thinking about?"

"How very much I love you," she answered without hesitation. A teasing smile feathered her lips. "And that I'd happily live in an empty refrigerator box under a bridge somewhere as long as you were there with me."

Though Marsh laughed, he dropped her case with a thud and strode to draw her into his arms. "While I seriously doubt that will ever be necessary, I'm both humbled and grateful to hear you say it."

If there had been so much as a tiny question in Jen's

mind about Marsh's declaration of love for her, hearing him admit to being humbled erased it forever.

Spearing her fingers into his hair, she thanked him with a searing kiss. Naturally, one kiss led to another, and then another, all the way into the house and up the stairs to his bedroom.

Physically and emotionally exhausted, they fell asleep still wrapped in each other's arms to sleep most of the next day away.

Over breakfast at seven that evening, dressed in Marsh's luxurious robe at his request, Jen listened to his suggestions for the holidays—and for planning their wedding.

First on his list was shopping for Jen. Then calling a friend of his...who just happened to be a judge.

They left early the next morning for San Antonio. Once in the city, they went their separate ways, agreeing to meet for lunch at the same restaurant along the River Walk where they had dined the previous time they had been there.

Excited about her venture, Jen went looking for the perfect wedding dress. Two hours into her search she found it. In what the saleslady referred to as "barely white," the dress was dressy but not formal. The filmy material clung to her upper body while the slightly flared skirt swirled around her legs just below her knees.

Her major purchase made, Jen set about looking for the perfect accessories. She decided on black pumps with three-inch heels along with a black clutch purse with a gold tone clasp. She chose a black pearl necklace with a matching bracelet and teardrop earrings.

The last—and to Jen the most important—purchase she made was a Christmas gift for Marsh. Delighted with her choices, she strolled along the River Walk to the restaurant. Marsh was waiting for her next to the entrance, a bemused smile on his face in response to her self-satisfied expression.

"You look very pleased with yourself, my love," he murmured, sweeping her into his arms right there in front of the world.

"I am," Jen said, giving him a quick kiss on the mouth. "I'm only a few minutes late."

His laughter ringing with the sound of happiness, Marsh ushered her into the restaurant.

"You spoke with the judge?" Jen asked anxiously the minute she was seated.

Marsh smiled. "Yes, he will be delighted to marry us at city hall the day before Christmas."

Jen sighed with satisfaction. "Good."

"Yes," he agreed. "Very good."

Later, over an after-dinner liqueur, Marsh reached for Jen's left hand. "I have a Christmas gift for you, but I can't wait. I want to give it to you now."

Jen began to tremble, almost certain she knew what it was—he *was* holding her left hand, after all.

She was right.

Reaching into his jacket pocket, Marsh drew out a small dark blue jeweler's box, opened it, then slid a large, many-faceted diamond solitaire engagement ring onto her finger.

"Oh, Marsh," she whispered. Without words, she let her misted eyes speak for her as, taking his hand, she brought it to her mouth to place a soft kiss on his palm.

"I guess that means you like it." His voice was rough with emotion.

"I love it," she said, "almost as much as I love you."

Jen waited until they were getting ready for bed that night before she presented him with the large boxed gift she had purchased. "I can't wait till Christmas, either."

Upon tearing away the festive wrap and whipping off the box lid, Marsh laughed as he pulled out an exact match to the terry robe he had given to her.

The last few remaining days before the holiday flew by. Jen and Marsh worked together during the day as they had before, he in his office, she in hers. She tidied the house and cooked the meals. He worked outside with the horses.

Although unchanged, the house looked barren to Jen. She longed for bright, glittering decorations. Marsh promised her he would help her deck every room of the house next Christmas…then surprised her with a small but fully decorated tree that he set in the center of the table.

Throughout those few days, being together was the same, yet different. There was a new depth of feeling, a sense of utter rightness and contentment that had been missing before. This time, they belonged together.

Jen called her mother on the day she and her father returned from their cruise. She offered a brief explanation of the situation between her and Marsh, and promised they would both be there for her mother's traditional family Christmas noontime brunch.

Christmas Eve day dawned bright and sunny. By midafternoon the weather was mild. Marsh was awed by the way she looked in her beautiful wedding dress, and she complimented him, for her husband-to-be looked devastatingly handsome in a charcoal-gray suit, white shirt and pearl-gray striped tie.

"One would think we were going to do something special," he remarked dryly as he helped her into the freshly washed and gleaming car.

"One would be correct," Jen agreed, her voice uneven due to the excited flutter of her heart.

"Then let's do it," he said, leaning in to kiss her cheek before starting the car.

At four-thirty in the afternoon the day before Christmas, it was quiet inside the Mission Alamo as two people stood, alone, together. As always, Jen was filled with a sensation of peace inside the structure. The very air they breathed held a sense of holiness. It was the perfect setting for their intentions.

They stood facing each other, arms at their sides, their hands tightly clasped.

"First off," Marsh began, "I swear to love you with every beat of my heart and every part of my body."

"And I," Jen replied, "I swear to love you with every beat of my heart and every part of my body."

He smiled before going on. "I, Marshall David Grainger, take thee, Jennifer Louise Dunning, for my lawfully wedded wife."

"I, Jennifer Louise Dunning, take you, Marshall David Grainger, for my lawfully wedded husband."

They were silent a moment. Both had wet eyes. Then Marsh drew Jen into his arms to hold her as if she were the most precious person in the world. Crying softly with joy, Jen wrapped her arms around his neck and clung as if she would never let him go.

Hand in hand, Marsh and Jen walked from the mission into the twilight of Christmas Eve.

Tugging gently on her hand, Marsh slanted a grin at her and said, "Now let's go see that judge."

"Yes, let's," she said, grinning back at him.

* * * * *

COMING NEXT MONTH from Harlequin Desire®

AVAILABLE APRIL 2, 2013

#2221 PLAYING FOR KEEPS
The Alpha Brotherhood
Catherine Mann

Malcolm Douglas uses his secret Interpol connections to protect his childhood sweetheart when her life is in danger. But their close proximity reignites flames they thought were long burned out.

#2222 NO STRANGER TO SCANDAL
Daughters of Power: The Capital
Rachel Bailey

Will a young reporter struggling to prove herself fall for the older single dad who's investigating her family's news network empire—with the intention of destroying it?

#2223 IN THE RANCHER'S ARMS
Rich, Rugged Ranchers
Kathie DeNosky

A socialite running from her father's scandals answers an ad for a mail-order bride. But when she falls for the wealthy rancher, she worries the truth will come out.

#2224 MILLIONAIRE IN A STETSON
Colorado Cattle Barons
Barbara Dunlop

The missing diary of heiress Niki Gerard's mother triggers an all-out scandal. While she figures out who she can trust, the new rancher in town stirs up passions...and harbors secrets of his own.

#2225 PROJECT: RUNAWAY HEIRESS
Project: Passion
Heidi Betts

A fashionista goes undercover to find out who's stealing her company's secrets but can't resist sleeping with the enemy when it comes to her new British billionaire boss.

#2226 CAROSELLI'S BABY CHASE
The Caroselli Inheritance
Michelle Celmer

The marketing specialist brought in to shake up Robert Caroselli's workaday world is the same woman he had a New Year's one-night stand with—and she's pregnant with his baby!

You can find more information on upcoming Harlequin® titles, free excerpts and more at www.Harlequin.com.

REQUEST YOUR FREE BOOKS!
2 FREE NOVELS PLUS 2 FREE GIFTS!

HARLEQUIN® *Desire*

ALWAYS POWERFUL, PASSIONATE AND PROVOCATIVE

SPECIAL EXCERPT FROM
HARLEQUIN® DESIRE

USA TODAY Bestselling Author

Catherine Mann

presents

PLAYING FOR KEEPS

Available April 2013 from Harlequin® Desire!

Midway through the junior high choir's rehearsal of "It's a Small World," Celia Patel found out just how small the world could shrink.

She dodged as half the singers—the female half—sprinted down the stands, squealing in fan-girl glee. All their preteen energy was focused on racing to where he stood.

Malcolm Douglas.

Seven-time Grammy Award winner.

Platinum-selling soft rock star.

And the man who'd broken Celia's heart when they were both sixteen years old.

Malcolm raised a stalling hand to his ominous body-guards while keeping his eyes locked on Celia, smiling that million-watt grin. Tall and honed, he still had a hometown-boy-handsome appeal. He'd merely matured—now polished with confidence and whipcord muscle.

She wanted him gone.

For her sanity's sake, she *needed* him gone. But now that he was here, she couldn't look away.

He wore his khakis and Ferragamo loafers with the easy confidence of a man comfortable in his skin. Sleeves rolled up on his chambray shirt exposed strong, tanned forearms and musician's hands.

Best not to think about his talented, nimble hands.

His sandy-brown hair was as thick as she remembered. It was still a little long, skimming over his forehead in a way that once called to her fingers to stroke it back. And those blue eyes—heaven help her…

There was no denying, he was all man now.

What in the hell was he doing here?

Malcolm hadn't set foot in Azalea, Mississippi, since a judge crony of her father's had offered Malcolm the choice of juvie or military reform school nearly eighteen years ago. Since he'd left her behind—scared, *pregnant* and determined to salvage her life.

But they weren't sixteen anymore, and she'd put aside reckless dreams the day she'd handed her newborn daughter over to a couple who could give the precious child everything Celia and Malcolm couldn't.

She threw back her shoulders and started across the gym.

She refused to let Malcolm's appearance yank the rug out from under her blessedly routine existence. She refused to give him the power to send her pulse racing.

She refused to let Malcolm Douglas threaten the future she'd built for herself.

What is Malcolm doing back in town?

Find out in

PLAYING FOR KEEPS

Available April 2013 from Harlequin® Desire!

HARLEQUIN® *Desire*

ALWAYS POWERFUL, PASSIONATE AND PROVOCATIVE.

When fashionista Lily Zaccaro goes undercover to find out who's stealing her company's secrets, she can't resist sleeping with the enemy, her new British billionaire boss, Nigel Statham.

Look for

PROJECT: RUNAWAY HEIRESS

by Heidi Betts

part of the
Project: Passion miniseries!

***Available April 2013 from Harlequin Desire
wherever books are sold.***

Project: Passion

On the runway, in the bedroom,
down the aisle—these high-flying
fashionistas mean business.

Powerful heroes…scandalous secrets…burning desires.